Forever Valley

FOREVER VALLEY

with an interview with Marie Redonnet

University of Nebraska Press: Lincoln & London

Marie Redonnet

TRANSLATED BY

JORDAN STUMP

© 1986 by Les Éditions de Minuit
Translation © 1994
by the University of Nebraska Press
All rights reserved
Manufactured in the United States
of America. The paper in
this book meets the minimum re-
quirements of American
National Standard for Information
Sciences – Permanence
of Paper for Printed Library Mater-
ials, ANSI z39.48-1984.
Library of Congress Cataloging-in-
Publication Data
Redonnet, Marie. [Forever valley.
English]
Forever valley / by Marie Redonnet:
with an Interview with
Marie Redonnet; translated by Jor-
dan Stump. p. cm.082. –
(European women writers series)
ISBN 0-8032-8951-0 (pa)
I. Series. PQ2678.E285F67   1995
843'.914 – dc20   94-1315   CIP

Contents

Forever Valley

To Paul Otchakovsky-Laurens

The roof of the church finally collapsed. The father said nothing. He lost interest in the church long ago, when it closed. It has been closed for as long as I can remember. The father does not have enough money to have the roof repaired anyway. Since the church is closed, what difference does it make? The church is empty. All the property of the church was sold at auction in the valley below. It was a good sale. The father made a little money from it. He has enough to live on, but he does not have enough to keep up the church. It is very old, it just barely holds together. Forever Valley is no longer a parish or a village, it is only a hamlet. The barns are empty and falling into ruins, like the church. It begins with the roof, and after that the whole thing falls apart. The valley below drew in the inhabitants of Forever Valley little by little. Now all of Forever Valley depends on the valley below. The parish, the municipal offices, the school, and the cemetery are down there.

I was raised by the father. The father is much too old to move to another parish. He was happy to be able to keep the rectory. He moved the harmonium into the rectory. That is all he has left from the church. The harmonium did not sell because it is an old model and it sounds bad. The father is very attached to the harmonium. It gives the rectory a furnished look. The father tried to teach me to play. I can play a few songs. The father must have raised me so I can look after him in his old age. He doesn't want to end up in the rest home. The home is his obsession.

4   Now that his legs are becoming paralyzed, he would have to leave the rectory and go to the home if I were not here. He has more and more difficulty walking. He leans against the walls. He can't even walk in his garden anymore. Massi bought him a wheelchair at an auction in the valley below. The father can no longer do without his wheelchair. He is very disappointed that he never managed to teach me to read. He must think I lack the necessary abilities. Not being able to read doesn't bother me, though. The father always reads the same book. What good would it do me to know how to read? I know perfectly well how to look after the father and the rectory. I do not want to leave Forever Valley. There is much too much traffic in the valley below because of the customs office. The border is just at the far end of the valley below. There is nothing at the end of Forever Valley, only the mountains. The end of Forever Valley is behind the hamlet. The hamlet is almost at the foot of the mountains. On one of the slopes, there is a very steep path that climbs up to the pass. They say that the pass is also the border. I have never been there. It doesn't tempt me. I would rather stay in the rectory. To climb up from the valley below to Forever Valley there is a gravel road. A gravel road with no outlet does not attract much traffic. Traffic is something that belongs in the valley below. I don't like traffic.

The father said it was Massi's turn to see to my education now that I have turned sixteen. Massi has always lived across from the rectory. She is like the father, she does not want to leave Forever Valley. And yet the father thought she would leave when her husband died. Her husband was someone. When he was young, he was at the same time the mayor and the schoolteacher of Forever Valley, back when there was a town hall and a school. And then there was no more school because there were no more children. But the town hall stayed open until the mayor died. Mayor was mostly an honorary title. There was not much to preside over, since the barns were empty. Massi was widowed young. On the facade of her house, it still says town hall and school. The school was the ground floor, and the second floor was the town hall. Massi has the words town hall and school repainted every so often. It looks strange now that it no longer means anything. Massi is proud to live in that house. It is a large house, out of proportion with the rest of the hamlet. The rectory looks tiny next to it. The father is pleased that Massi has the signs repainted. He says it reminds people that there used to be a town hall and a school in Forever Valley. He tried to teach me to read the words town hall and school, but I get them mixed up. I get all the words mixed up. Massi's husband is buried in the cemetery of the valley below, in the section reserved for the dead of Forever Valley. I used to go to the cemetery with Massi during the first year after her husband died. She wanted the grave of the mayor of

Forever Valley always to be covered with flowers. She was proud back then to have been the wife of the mayor. She had people call her Mrs. Mayoress. Now, no one calls her by her old title anymore. Massi did not have enough to live on when her husband died. She had never worked. The father thought she would leave. What could a woman her age do in Forever Valley? Massi had an enterprising mind. She did not want to abandon her house, the former town hall and former school. That was when she had the idea of opening the dancehall. Her house was too large for just her. None of the dancehalls in the valley below had any kind of reputation. Massi had everything in her house redone. Now the ground floor, where the classrooms were, is the main room of the dancehall. Massi had the walls torn down so the room would be very large. She also put in a little room to hang coats in, and an entryway where the customers pay. She put up a big sign in front of her house. She wrote DANCING on it in big capital letters. That is the only word I can read. Dancing is an easy word to read. Massi had made a name for herself in the valley below, back when she was the wife of the mayor of Forever Valley. Her reputation has grown since the dancehall opened. Massi has no reason to regret being widowed young. Her house was successful. On Saturday nights, the dancehall of Forever Valley attracts the herdsmen from the valley below and the customs officers from the customs office. Massi sells the tickets and runs the cash register herself. In one night she makes enough to live on for a week. She likes running the dancehall. She never seems to get older, and yet she has been widowed for a long time. The dancehall is directly across from the rectory, but the father never goes there, it is not suitable for someone in his position. But on Saturday nights he opens the rectory windows wide to listen to the music coming from the dancehall. That is the only night the harmonium is closed up. Massi bought herself the best gramophone available, and she has a stack of records. The dancehall is full of life and high spirits on Saturday nights. I always listen to the music from the gramophone with the father on Saturday nights. It is a kind of music that has nothing to do with the music of the harmonium.

I went to see Massi as the father asked, so she can see to my education. I still have not told the father about my personal project. If I did, he would think I am not old enough yet to see it through, and he would be opposed. Massi is all he ever talks about to me. Massi never goes to the cemetery anymore now that she has opened the dancehall. I have never been to Massi's on a Saturday night. I was not old enough before, and I don't know how to dance. Massi is very strict about rules. The dancehall is prohibited to anyone under sixteen. Maybe the father wants Massi to see to my education because I just turned sixteen and I can go to the dancehall on Saturday nights. Massi approved of the father's decision. She is happy that the father is sending me to her because she needs someone to help out on

Saturday nights. There are always the girls from the dairy in the valley below who work at the dancehall, but Massi says she can't count on them for everything. She told me she would introduce me to the customs officers. They are her preferred customers. She says I have a right to the best customers because the father gave me the best education. This is the first time Massi has shown me the second floor. There are a lot of bedrooms. It's much larger than the rectory. Massi let me into her room. There is a sign on the door. I asked what it said. It said: private. It does not seem to bother Massi that I don't know how to read. There is a large armoire in her room. Massi saw right away that I was looking at her armoire, and she opened it wide. The armoire is full of dresses. Massi picked one out and told me to try it on. It is an organdy dress, with flounces. I have never worn that kind of dress. In the rectory, I always wear an apron so that I don't get dirty. I don't know what to do with all these flounces. Massi said flounces look pretty when you dance. I don't dare move in my flounces. The neckline is not right for me, it hangs loose. Massi noticed that right away. I have never worn a low-cut dress. Massi says I have almost no bust, even though I should already be developed at my age. She put on her Saturday-night dress. It's not an organdy dress with flounces like mine. Massi says flounces do not suit women her age. It's a very straight dress, made of sateen, and slit on the sides. Organdy does not have the same effect as sateen, it's lighter and almost transparent. I like organdy. I am not used to flounces. Massi says it looks good on me, a dress with flounces makes me look more developed than I am. During the week, when the dancehall is closed, Massi makes dresses. She only has two styles. The straight slit sateen dresses are for the girls from the dairy who work at the dancehall. The organdy dresses with flounces are made especially for me, Massi says. There are two of them. Massi says you should always have a spare dress. The father never told me Massi made dresses. The rectory and the dancehall face each other, but they turn their backs to each other. All the windows of the rectory look out over the garden and the church. I don't know how old Massi is. She gave me shoes to go with my dress, patent leather high-heeled shoes. This is the first time I have worn high heels. They make me taller. A dress with flounces has to be worn with high heels. That's what Massi told me. She is right, high heels bring out the full effect of the flounces. She told me I could pay her later, I can have them on credit for now. So I am going to earn money. Massi said I would not regret coming to work at the dancehall. She seems to have a taste for business. She has a beautiful room. She must put everything she earns into furnishing and decorating the dancehall. It doesn't show from the outside. Even if you see the big sign that says dancing, you can't get an idea of the inside from the outside. It would be quite a surprise for the father. He has never been here. Massi showed me my room. She could see I was surprised, I didn't know I was going to have my own room at the

dancehall. She told me I would only use it on Saturday
nights. My room at the rectory looks very rudimentary
compared to my room at the dancehall. The father must
think I am old enough to earn a living for myself. There is
nothing but the dancehall in Forever Valley. In the valley
below, there is the dairy, but I couldn't work at the dairy
and look after the father at the same time. And also, the
dairy is right next to the road, and I don't like traffic. Massi
turned on the gramophone. She says she likes to dance,
and she will teach me how. She told me again that she
would introduce me to the customs officers when I was
ready. She has a high opinion of the customs officers. She
told me the customs officers don't like the girls from the
dairy. The girls from the dairy dance with the herdsmen.
Massi says she is getting too old to take care of all the
customs officers. That's why she is happy the father sent
me to work at the dancehall. She says the father raised me
well, and I am just right for the customs officers. I have
to come back and see her every day next week. She wants
to complete my education. I didn't really know Massi
before. She has more personality than I thought. She says
the future of Forever Valley is in the dancehall, and it is
only thanks to the dancehall that Forever Valley still has
life in it.

The father agreed with everything Massi said. He told me
to do just what she says, she knows what is right for me.
He wanted me to massage his legs. He seems to be in pain.

He looks old compared to Massi. He wanted me to play the harmonium for him. And then he wanted me to take him for a walk around the garden. He is proud of his garden. Forever Valley is nothing but rock, except in the rectory garden. The barns are empty now because there was nothing for the herds to live on. The father says there is an underground spring just under the rectory garden, and that is why the grass grows so tall and why there are all sorts of plants there that you never find anywhere else. Until just recently, the father used to spend all day working in the garden. The garden and the church in the middle of it is the most pleasant thing about the rectory. I call it a church to make the father happy, but really it is more of a chapel. It's much too little to be a church. Massi's house is impressive, but it has no garden. That must be why Massi does so much to decorate the inside. The rectory garden is surrounded by high walls. You are isolated from everything here. It's not easy to push the father's wheelchair in the garden. Massi could have checked the condition of the wheels before she bought it. The father is jolted this way and that in his wheelchair. He has twinges in his legs. He doesn't complain. He says if he has twinges, that is a sign that his legs are not really paralyzed yet. He wants me to take him for a walk despite the jolts.

I wondered for a long time whether or not I should tell the father about my personal project. If I did not tell him about it, I would never be able to see it through. I need his consent. And if I am old enough to spend Saturday nights at the dancehall, I am also old enough to see my personal project through. In the end I decided to tell the father about it. I told him I wanted to look for the dead. I have been thinking about it for a long time, ever since I went with Massi to the cemetery in the valley below to see the grave of the mayor of Forever Valley. I think there must be graves in Forever Valley as well. Why wouldn't there be, since there are graves in the valley below? There was a parish, a town hall, and a school in Forever Valley, why wouldn't there also have been a cemetery? I think the place to look for the dead would be the rectory garden. That is where they must be. In the valley below, the cemetery is just behind the church. If I want to see my project through I must have the father's consent. The garden is his domain. Overall, the father's reaction was favorable. All he asked was that I not mention it to Massi. He says she would never hire me at the dancehall if she knew I wanted to look for the dead. And the father wants me to work at the dancehall. He seemed to think long and hard about my project. He thinks he remembers that the archives of the valley below never mention a cemetery in Forever Valley. But the archives might not be old enough. The church is very old. There might very well have been a cemetery around the church in the old days. The father told me again not to say anything about this to Massi. She would not approve of my project. Why would I tell her? The dead have nothing to do with the dancehall. The father seems to look at me differently now that I have told him about my project. He must not have thought I could come up with my own project. He was disappointed that I never learned to read. But I don't need to know how to read to look for the dead. Maybe the father wants me to look for the dead. He doesn't know what to do anymore, with his legs half paralyzed. He did not want to talk about it any longer. He said it was time for bed. We go to bed early in the rectory. There is no generator like at Massi's. Everything is electric at Massi's. She says electricity is the greatest discovery of all time. She is proud of her generator. There is no electricity in the valley below, and no generator either. Massi wants the people below to see the dancehall on Saturday nights. That is why it's so brightly lit. Every evening, Massi's house lights up the hamlet. The rectory disappears into the shadows.

§2

I have spent every day this week at Massi's. I start work on Saturday night. That's very soon. Massi seems to be in a hurry for me to start. A week isn't much time to learn everything. Massi starts up the gramophone as soon as I get there, so she can teach me how to dance. She seems like a good dancer. She leads. I wouldn't know what to do if she were not there. She told me to let myself be led. I step on her feet. She shows me what to do to please the customs officers. I will only dance with the customs officers. She seems set on that. I have to get used to the gramophone music. Maybe it was listening to harmonium music all the time that gave me the idea of looking for the dead. The harmonium makes me think of the dead. I do not know if I would have had the idea of looking for the dead if all I had ever listened to was gramophone music. Massi wants me to wear high heels when I dance. It's not easy to dance when you are not used to it. I lose my balance when I dance with high heels on. Massi keeps her floor brightly polished. When you dance on it, you slide along effortlessly. Massi says a well-waxed floor is essential for a dancehall. Her dancehall is in the highest category. She says I am too stiff when I dance. But I do just what she tells me. She redid the neckline on my dress so it would not hang loose. This time, the dress really fits me. I wanted to go show the father. That would have been a surprise for him, he would not have recognized me. Massi would not allow it. She said the father has no interest in dresses, he isn't able to appreciate them and I would be disturbing him for nothing. Dresses are Massi's concern, not the father's. I don't want to disobey her. She must be right. The only thing the father wants to know when I get back from the dancehall is whether Massi is happy with me, whether she thinks I am capable of working at the dancehall on Saturday nights. The father isn't curious about the rest of it. He has never been curious. He never leaves the rectory. Massi says soon I won't be so stiff. I asked her if she had already had the idea of running a dancehall back when her husband was alive. She said no, she could not have been the wife of the mayor and school-teacher of Forever Valley and run a dancehall at the same time. She has had two lives, in a way. When I go to her house, she is always busy sewing or polishing the floor of the dancehall. I never knew how much you had to polish a floor to make it look that way. And it's incredible how shiny it is. You almost want to look at yourself in it. Every time I go there, Massi tells me she is happy I just turned sixteen, because she needs me to help out at the dancehall. It is as if the father raised me knowing I would go to work at the dancehall. Dancing every day to get ready for Saturday night is giving me sore legs. Massi says it's good for my development. She puts on all sorts of records. She teaches me to dance the different dances. There is much more variety with a gramophone than with a harmonium. No matter how many different songs you play, it's always the same song when you play the harmonium.

Massi also explained what I will have to do when I go up to my room with one of the customs officers. That's why I have my own room. Massi says all I have to do is let things happen, the customs officers know what to do. She checked me to make sure I was anatomically normal. She says I'm normal, I am just behind in my development. The father never talked to me about my anatomy or my development. Massi says that's not his job. She says not being developed is really nothing to complain about. The customs officers will not complain either, since they won't have to take precautions. Massi explains everything to me, my anatomy, my development. She explained that it is

better when the customs officers don't have to take precautions. They pay a higher price and I make more money. She showed me all the tickets to the dancehall in the drawer of her cashier's box. There are all different colors, some for the herdsmen and some for the customs officers. The pink tickets are for the herdsmen who do nothing but dance with the girls from the dairy. Those are the least expensive. The blue tickets are for the ones who do nothing but go to the rooms. The green tickets are for the ones who want to dance first and then go up to a room with one of the girls from the dairy. The yellow tickets and the white tickets are the most expensive, they are only for the customs officers. Both kinds of tickets let them dance and go to the rooms. The yellow tickets are for when the customs officers have to take precautions. The white tickets are the most expensive, they are for when they don't have to take precautions. Those are the customs officers' favorites. Massi thought she would have to sell yellow tickets for me. She is happy that it will be white tickets. The customs officers buy white tickets for her too, because she is past the age when they have to take precautions with her. That's what she explained to me. All in all, she is thrilled that I am not developed yet. She is very organized. All her tickets are carefully put away in the drawer, the herdsmen's on one side and the customs officers' on the other. She can't get them mixed up. She likes the dance-

hall, but she likes business too. She said the customs officers always want to dance before they go up to a room.
That's why I have to know how to dance. With the customs officers, the room always comes after dancing. Everything Massi told me is getting mixed up in my head. It
is all new to me, the dancehall, my development, what I
have to do with the customs officers in my room. Until
now, I never knew I wasn't developed yet. The father always acted as if everything was perfectly normal, except
that I don't know how to read. To Massi, it must be as
important to be developed as it is to know how to read.
Massi doesn't want me to talk to the father about all this. I
am nervous about Saturday night. With Massi everything
seems easy, but I don't know the customs officers. Massi
wanted me to look in the big mirror in my room to see my
anatomy, so I could really understand all her explanations.
I had never looked at myself before. In the rectory, there is
only a little mirror for looking at your face. In my room at
the dancehall, there is also a bathroom with all the conveniences. Massi explained that it was important to know
just what to do in the bathroom. She showed me what to
do. She said I had to wash myself as soon as I was finished
with a customs officer. I have never washed myself so carefully. Massi says I am at the age where I should wash carefully. She has always taken care of herself, and that's why
she does not look her age. She says the girls from the dairy
are not careful enough, so the customs officers never want
to go up to the rooms with them. My head is spinning

from thinking about everything Massi told me. The father raised me in ignorance.

Every day, Massi pays a short visit to the father. This is the first time I have been allowed to stay for one of her visits. Until now, the father always told me to go to my room. That's a sign that I am grown up. Massi brought the father a cake. She made it herself, she knows how much the father likes treats. The father ate the whole thing right away. I understand why he never has any dessert at dinner. He is waiting to have his dessert when Massi comes. He knows she never forgets to bring it. That's also why the father calls me at night and asks me to make him some herb tea, his stomach is too full. Ever since his legs started becoming paralyzed, his entire body has been getting weaker. He pushes himself too hard trying to walk around the rectory. It's not good for his stomach. He should give up walking. He should also give up Massi's treats, they only make things worse. Massi has been too indulgent with the father. She let him fall into bad habits. He would miss it now if Massi stopped bringing him his cake. Massi and the father talked about the money the dancehall took in the week before. I was surprised. The father told Massi her money would bear fruit thanks to him, that it was only a question of finding the best investments. Now that Massi has decorated and furnished her dancehall, she gives her money to the father to invest. Massi knows nothing about investments. She leaves it all up to the father. The father tells Massi he knows just what to do. I would never have thought he knew anything about investments. Maybe I had also better give him the money I make at the dance-hall so he can make it bear fruit. I don't know why Massi wears herself out sewing all week. She could live just on what she makes at her dancehall. Massi and the father talked about nothing but investments. I did not understand much. I didn't even know it was possible to make your money bear fruit.

My personal project is not a moneymaking project. I am lucky the father isn't opposed to it. I could not live without my project. I have not even had time to think about the dead this week. I am too preoccupied by Saturday night. I have to be able to do everything Massi has been teaching me. She has faith in me, and she is counting on me. The father is taking advantage of my preoccupation to think about the dead in my place. You can tell it from his behavior, which is not the same as usual. He even told me he would guide me as I look for the dead. I don't want him to guide me. It is my project, not his. I even had a bad thought. I almost told myself it was a good thing the father's legs are becoming paralyzed. That way I will be on my own, I can be sure he won't be able to look with me. You have to have solid legs to look for the dead. And he can hardly take three steps before he has to sit down in his wheelchair. Massi should not bring him such big treats. It's not good for his paralysis. The father should be thinking about the dead instead of Massi's money. What matters most is that I look for the dead.

Every evening when I come home from Massi's, I take the father into the garden for his walk. The garden is not kept up as well as it used to be. It's full of smells because of all the plants and also because of the evening dew. The rectory garden is the only place in Forever Valley where the dew falls in the evening. Everywhere else, it is too dry. The father says the underground spring stays buried in the earth rather than flowing into the stream bed. In the summer, there is never any water in the stream bed. I tried to fix the wheels of the wheelchair. Massi bought a bad wheelchair. The church has not improved since the roof collapsed. There are stones falling from the walls. Soon the church will be like the barns. The walls are not solid at all anymore. Instead of investing all her money, Massi could make a donation for the church. The church is also part of the hamlet. The father does not give her good advice. Instead of asking Massi to make a donation for the church, he talks about investments. The church makes a bad impression in the state it's in. It spoils the view of the garden. The father takes no notice. The church, the garden, the rectory, they all go together. I don't understand why the father is so indifferent about the condition of the church. The dancehall is the only building in Forever Valley that is being kept up. The church of the valley below is the opposite of the one in Forever Valley, it is always being restored. It's just by the road, across from the dairy. I went inside once. It's noisy because of the traffic, and it smells like the dairy. I don't like that smell. I can see why the father has always preferred his garden to the valley below. I prefer the rectory garden too. The dead occupy the father's mind. They make him forget that his legs are becoming paralyzed. He never talks about Massi or the dancehall anymore. Maybe his paralysis will even be slowed down if he feels optimistic about finding the dead.

§3

Saturday night came even more quickly than I expected. Even after the training Massi gave me all week long, I still didn't feel ready. I felt nervous all day. The father wanted me to play the harmonium. He seems to be trying to take over my project. He is forgetting that the dancehall is not the only thing on my mind. He tried to get up out of his wheelchair, and he fell down. He hurt his head, he hit his head when he fell. His legs won't hold him anymore. He must be trying to take over my project so he can forget about his legs. Playing the harmonium did nothing to calm my nerves. I played a lot of wrong notes. The father was not happy. But if his ear was as sensitive as he claims, he would never have been able to put up with that harmonium all this time. No one wanted anything to do with it at the auction, not even at the lowest prices. I have never been to the dancehall on a Saturday night.

The father did not ask me to open the windows as I left the rectory. So he doesn't want to listen to the music coming from the dancehall. And yet usually he listens to it every Saturday night. Massi does not visit him on Saturdays, she is too busy with other things to make him his cake or to come see him. So in a way the gramophone music makes up for the treat he didn't get, which he misses. I do not know why he doesn't want to listen to it tonight. He is becoming withdrawn. I got to Massi's early so I would have plenty of time to get ready. Massi was already wearing her straight slit sateen dress. She put on a pearl necklace the same color as her dress. The neckline shows her bust to its best advantage. Massi knows how to show herself to her best advantage. She says that's important at her age. My bust is nothing at all next to Massi's. Massi told me the bust is not the only thing that matters. The proof is that the girls from the dairy are very busty, much more than Massi, and yet none of the customs officers want anything to do with them. Massi did my hair, she gave me curls. I looked at myself in the mirror. I thought my organdy dress really suited me now that Massi had redone the neckline. I can't be compared to Massi. We are not the same age.

The girls from the dairy who work at the dancehall on Saturday nights arrived early. Massi introduced me to them. They have that dairy smell I noticed in the valley below when I went into the church. I don't like it. And yet they wear a lot of perfume. But that brings out the smell even more. They don't have much style. Massi says they have just the right style for the herdsmen from the valley below. They wear straight slit sateen dresses like Massi. But the dress is not as stylish on them as on Massi. It looks cheap. They must drink a lot of milk to have such white skin. Massi told me I didn't know what I was talking about, and that they were wonderful girls. They hardly looked at me. They must not have thought much of me in my organdy dress with flounces. They went right off to their rooms to get ready. They are impatient for the dancehall to open. They want to earn enough money to be able to leave the dairy. Massi never has to look for girls. When one of them goes away, there is always another who volunteers to replace her. Massi can afford to be demanding. For her, the dairy is a source of employees. I am nothing like the girls from the dairy. I am the only one wearing an organdy dress with flounces. I am used to all the flounces on my dress. It is more practical for dancing than a straight dress, even a slit one. It's lighter too, it doesn't stick to the skin. Massi turned on the gramophone. She turned on all the lights. On Saturday nights, all the lights in the dancehall are turned on. Massi says it looks modern. She likes everything modern. As soon as night fell, the line started to form in front of the cashier's box where Massi sits. She sold a lot of tickets, in every color.

The four customs officers were there too. The customs office is closed on Saturday nights just so all the customs officers can enjoy the dancehall. That was a personal initiative of the head customs officer. The fourth customs officer is a new one, a probationary officer. Massi doesn't know him. Last Saturday she said goodbye to his predecessor, who was appointed to a more important office. That is the dream of all the customs officers of the valley below, to be appointed to a more important office. Massi introduced me right away. They all bought white tickets, except the head officer. The dancehall is like home to him. He never pays to get in. Massi never told me he was allowed special privileges. He is the senior officer. He was appointed customs officer the same year Massi opened her dancehall. Then he was named head customs officer by seniority. He hardly looked at me. Massi took care of him right away. He is the dancehall's oldest customer. He and Massi went right up to her room, without even dancing. That goes against everything Massi taught me, that the customs officers always dance before they go up to the room. It must be because of the head customs officer that Massi needs me to help out at the dancehall. She no longer wants to take care of anyone but him. The regular customs officers are for me now. She didn't tell me I would have to take care of three customs officers all by myself. She showed me the one I had to dance with first. They are signed up in a certain order. I have to stick to the order. Massi does not like disorder, she has a list of customers for each room. When I have finished with the first customs officer, I will take care of the second. The probationary officer is written in last.

I danced with the first customs officer the way Massi has been teaching me all week. I don't know if it was because he thought I was too stiff when I danced, but he was in a hurry to go up to my room. Right away, he gave me the two white tickets he had bought from Massi. I asked him why he had two tickets. He said it was because he was the first one to go up to my room with me. Tonight, the fee is doubled for the first customs officer who goes upstairs with me, because this is my first night at the dancehall. From now on, it will only be one ticket. I did what Massi told me to do, she explained everything just right, there were no surprises. The first customs officer hurt me a little, Massi said it would hurt a little, I am not soft, it didn't hurt much, and the first customs officer knew what he was doing, it didn't take long. I went and washed myself right away when he was done, just as Massi told me. There was almost no blood. I was feeling a little dazed. The first customs officer told me his name was Fred. This is the only time I will get two white tickets at the same time. Officer Fred seemed pleased when he went back down to the dancehall. Then I danced with the second customs officer. He was waiting his turn sitting on a bench. He wanted to dance for a long time, one dance after another, without ever stopping. I still need practice. I was out of breath from dancing so long. My legs hurt, and I was sweating like I have never sweated before. It gets very hot in the dancehall on Saturday nights. It doesn't matter that Massi bought the very latest model of electric fans, the fans only stir up the hot air. I have sweat stains on my organdy dress from dancing with the second customs officer. Sweat stains are hard to get out, particularly from organdy. Organdy is a very delicate fabric. I am very upset that I stained my dress. The second customs officer didn't care about the sweat stains spreading over my dress, all he could think about was dancing. I was completely worn out from dancing so long. I looked around the room trying to catch a glimpse of Massi, but I didn't see her. She must still have been in her room with the head customs officer. She has all the time she wants now that I am dividing myself among all the customs officers. When the second customs officer told me to go up to my room, I was very happy to stop dancing. He was not the least bit tired. He told me his name right away. His name is Ted. He wants me to call him Ted all the time. He likes his name a lot. It is easy to pronounce and to remember, I had no trouble pronouncing it. It lasted as long up in the room with officer Ted as it did down on the dance floor. He must have made Massi impatient when she took care of him. Now she doesn't need to be impatient anymore, she has the whole evening to herself and the head customs officer. The mirror is just across from the bed. I could see everything officer Ted was doing. It gave me something to do to look in the mirror, it was interesting, I saw everything officer Ted was doing. This time, it didn't hurt. It is easier the second time, that's just what Massi told me. Officer Ted gave me his white ticket right at the end.

He seemed pleased. Neither officer Fred nor officer Ted seemed to miss Massi. I was afraid they would miss her. I am not experienced like she is. This is my first Saturday at the dancehall.

My evening was not over yet. I had to take care of the third customs officer, the probationary officer. He doesn't know how to dance, this is the first time he has been to a dance-hall. I had to teach him. I did exactly what Massi taught me to teach him how to dance. But he is stiffer than I am, he doesn't listen to the music. He stepped on my feet all the time, and he scuffed my patent leather shoes. Massi had not warned me that there would be customs officers who don't know how to dance. But then she doesn't know the probationary officer, he is a newcomer at the customs office. Since I was tired of dancing and could see he was not enjoying it, and since he seemed hesitant about asking me to go up to my room, I finally suggested it myself. He followed me without saying anything. When we got to my room, he fainted. I wanted to go find Massi. She didn't explain what I should do in a situation like this. Maybe this has never happened to her. But Massi still wasn't downstairs. There was no one to help me, downstairs everyone was dancing, and in the rooms they were busy. Massi told me never to disturb people when they are busy in the rooms. It must be the altitude that made him feel faint. He is not used to the mountains yet. I laid him down on the bed. I fanned him. He did not wake up until the

very end, when the music from the gramophone stopped. I don't know if the music might also have made him feel
faint. Maybe I made him dance too much, he got dizzy, and then it's so hot too. I got a sore wrist from fanning him constantly to help wake him up so he could do what the others did. He paid for a white ticket. But when he came around it was too late, the dancehall was closing. He remembered to give me his white ticket, but he forgot to tell me his name. He was very pale. The dancehall was not a success for him. He left without getting any good out of his white ticket. I didn't tell anyone he had lost consciousness. That would not have looked good. He doesn't want to make a bad impression. A probationary officer has to prove himself. And Massi might have thought I didn't know what I was doing.

Finally Massi and I were alone again. The dance floor is all scratched. It will take a great deal of polishing to get it back in shape. The girls from the dairy are careless, everything is in a mess. Massi seems tired, her dress is rumpled, she looks her age all of a sudden. Even just one customs officer is a lot for her. She asked me to tell her all about it. I said nothing about the probationary customs officer. I wouldn't want her to tell the head officer, she probably tells him everything. I gave her my four white tickets. In return, she gave me the money I had earned. I would not earn this much at the dairy in a week, and I wouldn't be able to bear the smell, I would faint like the probationary officer did in my room. This first Saturday went well. That is what I told Massi. I have the necessary abilities to work at the dancehall. The customs officers took to me easily. To me, a customs officer is a customs officer. The only difference is that with officer Ted it lasts longer than with officer Fred, but that is part of my work, I have to work all evening.

The father was waiting for me when I came back. I thought he wanted me to tell him all about my night at the dancehall. He only wanted to know how much I had made. He said it was a tidy sum, and he asked me to give it to him. I gave it to him without arguing. I didn't feel like arguing. Afterwards, he left me alone. I don't mind giving him my money to invest. I would not know what to do with it. There is nothing to buy in Forever Valley, and I don't like to go down to the valley below. The father is willing to let me look for the dead, as long as I give him the money I make at the dancehall. I thought about the customs officers again. The probationary officer does not seem sure of himself like the other officers. He doesn't seem to be in very good health either. The customs office is not working out for him. The father can become as paralyzed as he wants. I don't trust him anymore. He wants the dead just for himself. He is willing to let me look for them, but only so he can take them from me afterwards. And Massi wants to unload onto me everything she no longer wants to do with the customs officers. Three customs officers in one night is a lot, even if the probation-ary officer lost consciousness. I don't share Massi's taste for customs officers. The head officer is an officer like any other, except that he has more seniority on the job. What makes the dancehall such a success is the rooms upstairs. The dancehall in the valley below only has a ground floor. Massi knew how to take advantage of the second floor of her house. It was the town hall and the school, that's why it has a second floor. Massi knows what to do. She owes her reputation to her old title of mayoress. Even if no one calls her Mrs. Mayoress anymore, it still makes an impres-sion. Part of the dancehall's reputation comes from the fact that it used to be the school and the town hall of Forever Valley. The father thinks he can do as he pleases because he knows I will not leave him. I don't want to leave him because I want to look for the dead in the rec-tory garden. The father thinks he knows all there is to know about the dead.

§4

Now that I work at the dancehall on Saturday nights, I can do what I like with my Sundays. I need a day to rest up from Saturday night. One night at the dancehall made me more tired than I have ever been before. It's a good thing it is open only one night a week, I would never be able to work several nights in a row. I am not sorry I was raised at the rectory. It gives me a special position at the dancehall. And I am free all week. Looking after the father is not much fun, but I have time to think about my project. The girls from the dairy who work at the dancehall on Saturday nights are old before their time. They must not be a pretty sight by the time they have saved up enough money to leave the dairy. In the end, the father knows nothing at all about the dead. He is depending on me. He must think I have a plan since it is my project. He is wrong, I don't have a plan. But I have my instincts. And it is better to have instincts than to have a plan. I commandeered the father's garden tools. He can't use them anymore since he is condemned to immobility because of his legs. The tools that interest me are the large shovel and the little pick. I need a shovel and a pick to look for the dead. I am going to begin by digging a pit. If the dead are in the garden, they can only be found by digging pits. Over time, they have become invisible. I can't guess where they are. I am going to start digging on the north, just behind the church. That is where the dead are in the valley below, just behind the church. I won't be seen digging from the rectory. I would rather the father did not see me. It will do me good to dig. I need exercise. I have to get toughened up. I am too delicate. Just dancing a few dances in a row with officer Ted was enough to wear me out. I will begin by digging a small pit so I don't exceed my abilities. I have never dug a pit before.

I marked out the rectangle I am going to dig up, and then I pulled up the weeds so it would be very neat where I dig.

It's not a little thing to begin digging a pit, especially for the first time. I started working with the pick, because the pick is easier to handle than the shovel. I had barely started when I heard the father calling me. He is on the alert for any noise, and he recognized the sound of his pick right away. He wanted to know what I was up to in the garden. He can't leave me alone. He wants to be kept informed about everything. He wanted to know what I was doing with his pick. I had to tell him I was digging my first pit. He thought it was a good idea. He doesn't want to stay in the rectory while I look for the dead. I told him it was very hot in the garden because of the bright sunlight. But he didn't want to hear about it. He said he would put on his hat. It is an old gardener's hat which has lost its shape. It's not his size, it falls down over his forehead, it barely stays on. The father says it is a good hat and that he will be well protected from the sun. I pushed his wheelchair over to where I am working. The father says he wants to be where I am digging so he can keep an eye on everything I do. There is nothing I can say, it is his garden. I noticed that he has stopped saying he wants to guide me. He realizes he would not be able to. He wouldn't know how to go about it if he was the one who was looking for the dead. He wanted me to push his wheelchair forward so he would be right by the edge of the pit. It must hurt him to be reduced to watching, when he used to be so good at using a pick and shovel. He must be thinking he didn't make very good use of them, that it would have been better for him to look for the dead instead of only keeping the garden free of weeds. The shovel is heavy for me. The shovel was just right for the father back when he was in his prime. It puts a strain on my arms. The pick is lighter, but I can't dig just with a pick, I would never get anywhere. I have to dig with the shovel. When it's full, I can just barely lift it. I have to stop all the time. The ground is hard because it is summer and it doesn't rain. After a while, I started running into stones. I have always said Forever Valley is full of stones. In Forever Valley stones are easier to find than the dead. It's not a little thing to dig a pit. It doesn't go quickly, especially since I have to keep an eye on the father at the same time as I dig. He leans forward too far to see what I am doing, and when he leans forward too far, his hat falls off. I have to pick it up, otherwise the father would get sunstroke. He would never be able to withstand sunstroke in his condition. He is worked up. You would almost think he was the one doing the digging. He says I don't know how to handle the shovel, and if it was him he would almost be finished digging the pit by now. That's easy to say sitting in a wheelchair. I even put a cushion behind his back so he would be more comfortable. I wouldn't want him to get a sore back, with his legs already hurting. The father keeps slowing me down. He is impatient for me to find something. I told him I was digging without a plan. There is no reason to think I will find the dead in my first pit. He told me to go faster, he said I don't know how to get into a rhythm with the shovel. I already have blisters on my hands. It was a good idea to dig behind the church. When Massi comes to see the father in the rectory, there is no chance of her seeing the pit. I don't want her to know. Still, there is no reason to be afraid she would want me to leave the dancehall, even if she found out I am looking for the dead. She needs me to take care of the customs officers for her. She has never had any interest in the rectory garden. She says it's full of insects, and she doesn't want the insects to bite her. She wants to keep her skin unmarked. She is an indoors woman. She lives closed up in her dancehall. I have to be careful of insects too now. I must not let myself be bitten. The customs officers wouldn't like it if my skin was covered with insect bites.

Massi's visit was short, and yet the father did not complain. Normally, he always complains that Massi's visits are too short, even when they are much longer than today's. Massi had good things to say about me, she told him I was just right for the dancehall. The father was happy. He is the one who raised me, he thinks he raised me well. All Massi did was give me some further education, and only for a week. The important part was all the father's doing. He must be starting to have a higher opinion of me. Even if I don't know how to read, I still have abilities. Massi was in a hurry to leave. I saw her go off in the direction of the valley below. Usually she spends her afternoons sewing, she doesn't go down to the valley below. She must be going to the customs office. The head customs officer has a break in the afternoon, and Massi goes to join him. Maybe she wants to have a steady relationship. She thinks she can allow herself that luxury now that I am helping out at the dancehall. Maybe that's why she asks the father to invest her money for her. She is thinking of starting over a third time. Even though she was in a hurry to leave, she still remembered to give the father his two cakes. She knows how important that is to the father. He gets a double helping on Mondays because he hasn't had any for two days. He is a glutton. He ate it all up almost in one bite. I thought he would leave me alone after Massi left. Normally, he wants to be alone after she leaves. But this time he wanted to go back to the pit right away. And yet it was the worst time of day, when the sun is at its strongest. The father will not take any precautions. I don't know why he is in such a hurry. You have to be patient when you are looking for the dead. He runs the risk of being disappointed if he is in too much of a hurry. Furthermore, he was wrong to want to come out to the garden with me right after Massi left. He ate up his treat too quickly. Out in the sun, his stomach started to hurt, and he felt nauseous. He had to give up on the pit. I brought him right back into the rectory, and put him to bed. That will be a lesson to him. He was sick again and again. From now on, he won't eat up his treat in one breath, he will learn to chew thoroughly. He is not as resistant as he used to be. This was a warning to him. What would become of him without me?

The next day, the father was feeling badly. His stomach was not bothering him anymore, but he was generally out of sorts. I put him on a liquid diet. Massi came by, in a hurry. She is going down to the customs office again. I could tell from her clothes, which she had chosen with great care. I don't know why she singled out the head customs officer. He doesn't have anything the others don't have. Massi hardly noticed that the father was feeling badly. He took his cake from her all the same. Massi had not forgotten it. He didn't eat it because he is on a liquid diet, but he said he would have two to eat tomorrow. He didn't notice what a hurry Massi was in to leave. He is much too preoccupied by his discomfort, which is keeping him from the pit. I wanted to go dig while he rested. He would not allow it. He said I should only dig with him present. Even if I am sixteen years old and I work at the dancehall, I cannot disobey the father. It was a long afternoon watching over the father in the semidarkness of the rectory. He wanted me to play the harmonium. He must have thought time was dragging by too. It always does him good to hear music from the harmonium. I don't know why I played so badly. I was playing the songs I know best. I played one wrong note after another. This time it is not nervousness, today isn't Saturday. The father seemed unhappy to hear me playing so many wrong notes. He said I was forgetting what he had taught me. The harmonium really does not have a very nice sound. How could the father stand it, when he is so proud of his good taste? He must secretly think that going to the dancehall on Saturday nights is making me forget his lessons. He can't criticize me for that, he was the one who wanted me to go. Really, when it comes to the sound, there is no comparison between the gramophone and the harmonium. Massi always buys the best, whereas the father skimps on everything. He certainly would not give me an organdy dress with flounces. Massi didn't give me one either. I owe her for it, along with my patent leather high heels. She will take it out of my white tickets next time. No one gives me anything.

A day on a liquid diet did the father some good. Now he does everything the reverse of the way he used to. He takes his treat out to the garden and savors it by the pit, letting it melt in his mouth as slowly as possible. Massi's visits get shorter and shorter. She never tells me any secrets. I never tell her any either. She knows nothing about my activities during the week. She tells me I should get plenty of rest, and that I should use my time to become even more pleasing to the customs officers. I am pleasing enough to them as it is. My arms are sore from digging so much with the father's shovel, which wasn't meant for me. On Sunday I had sore legs from dancing so much on Saturday night, and this week I have sore arms from digging so much. My body is becoming built up. I like digging. I am past the stones now, the dirt I am digging in is almost loose. The father says it's because of the underground spring. Starting at a certain depth, it has a beneficial effect on the soil of the garden. My first pit already looks like a real pit. The only thing missing is the dead. I have done a good job of digging, I almost disappear when I am in the pit. The father has to lean further and further forward if he wants to watch me dig. It is dangerous for him to lean, his balance is not so good anymore. I wonder if I am going to find the dead in this pit. It would be a miracle if I found them in my first pit. The father wants me to keep digging. He says the dead must be buried very deep because they have been there for a very long time. His reasoning is confused. There is no connection. But I am willing to dig a little more.

In the evening, I am too tired to wheel the father around the garden. He doesn't insist, because he is tired from having spent the whole day in front of the pit. His legs are hard. They are completely paralyzed. The father can't stand up alone anymore. I have to help him get into bed. He is heavy. He has back pains from sitting all day. No matter how many cushions I give him, his back still hurts. The wheelchair Massi chose really isn't comfortable. I don't understand why she was so careless, when she always buys the very best. Fortunately the father has the pit to keep him occupied. Massi's visits are over as soon as they begin. She has changed her hair color. It doesn't go with her pale complexion at all. It almost makes her look like one of the girls from the dairy, but Massi is older. Why does she want to change her appearance? She used to look so elegant. The only reason the father looks forward to Massi's visits now is because of the cake. But since she started going down to the valley below every day, Massi gives him store-bought cakes. The father noticed right away, he didn't think it tasted good. He prefers the cakes Massi makes to the store-bought ones she gets in the valley below. He did not dare tell her, for fear she would stop bringing them. He likes the store-bought cakes better than nothing.

§5

The second Saturday, I was less nervous. I only worked in the garden in the morning, so I could rest all afternoon while I waited for it to be time to go to the dancehall. I had to give up on the first pit. The father was forced to accept that the dead were not there. My shovel hit solid rock all of a sudden. If I had continued, I would have broken the shovel. Without the shovel, I wouldn't be able to go on digging the other pits. The father knows it. The rock at the bottom of the first pit is the same as you find in the mountains overlooking Forever Valley. The father didn't expect to find rock at that depth. He was expecting to find the dead. He was unhappy that I didn't want to work in the garden that afternoon. He would have liked me to start digging the second pit right away. He asked me to push his wheelchair over to the harmonium. He played all afternoon, as if he wanted to keep me from resting. When evening came, he didn't ask me to open the windows. It seems like he lost interest in the music from the gramophone when I started working at the dancehall. I don't know why the father is in such a hurry for me to find the dead. I have always told him it would take time. I still don't have much experience digging pits. The father never reads his book anymore. He has lost interest in everything that isn't the dead. I tried to massage his legs before I left for the dancehall. He complained that I didn't know how to give a massage. I didn't dare tell him that with his legs in the condition they are in, massages will not do any good anymore. He never even talked to Massi about her investments this week. Massi's mind must really be on something else for her not to notice that the father's mind is also on something else. I don't care if the father has lost interest in investments. Massi will just have to look after her investments herself. She had no trouble getting the dancehall started, even though it was a town hall and a school at the beginning. Not everyone would have been capable of that.

When I got to the dancehall, Massi had not waxed the floor. She told me she was out of wax and the supply had run out in the valley below. She can say what she likes. She has always had extra wax stored up for just this kind of situation. The dancehall of Forever Valley is known for its well-waxed floor. It is hard to keep up, of course, and Massi has had other things to think about this week besides polishing her floor. This is not good for the dance-hall's reputation. With her new hair color, Massi isn't the same anymore, especially when she is wearing her straight slit sateen dress. I don't know what kind of style she has anymore. She always told me the customs officers don't like the style of the girls from the dairy. I don't know what she is after. She hasn't washed my organdy dress. And yet I thought that was her responsibility. I don't know how to wash such a fragile dress, or how to iron all those flounces. My dress is dirty, with all the sweat stains from last week. It's not wearable. There is a second organdy dress with flounces in Massi's armoire. It's not really my size, because the neckline hangs loose. Massi deliberately didn't wash my dress so I would have to buy the other dress she keeps in her armoire. That is going to double my debt. I tried on the second dress. The flounces have more sizing. Massi made a stitch on each side so the neckline wouldn't hang. The second dress fits me as well as the first now that Massi touched it up, and the flounces stay in place better than last Saturday because they have more sizing. I don't regret having a spare dress.

The girls from the dairy arrived at the same time as last Saturday. Their skin has a yellow tinge, when last week it was so white. I couldn't stop myself from asking them what was wrong. They said the herds in the valley below are sick. They have milk fever. The girls didn't realize it in time, and they drank tainted milk. It damaged their livers.

That's why they look yellow. They are wearing rouge to hide it, but it is even more noticeable. The rouge brings out the yellow. They don't look at ease. All that milk going bad is not good for the dairy. And the herdsmen are worried about their herds. They spent a lot on medicine. The girls from the dairy are worried that the herdsmen will hold back tonight and only buy pink tickets, since those are the least expensive tickets. They also say the atmosphere in the valley below is tense. The herdsmen are blaming the customs office and all the traffic it brings in. They say the customs officers are not checking the traffic carefully enough, and that's why the herds are sick. Massi went down to the valley below every day this week, she could have kept me informed. She must be worried about the head customs officer. The girls from the dairy think I am a privileged creature who knows nothing about life. They keep me at arm's length. My skin is not yellow like theirs, it's tan from all those hours I spent in the sun digging the first pit. The customs officers have fixed salaries. They will buy the same white tickets as usual. They are not affected by the sickness in the herds. That's what the girls from the dairy think. I have nothing to do with them. It's not my fault they are unattractive to the customs officers and they appeal only to the herdsmen. No matter how much Massi tries to look like one of them, she still has her creamy complexion. She hasn't drunk any tainted milk. She is like me, she never drinks milk. She did everything the way she does every Saturday night. She turned on the gramophone. She turned on all the lights. She sat down in the cashier's box.

This is not a Saturday night like the others, undoubtedly because of the disease that is souring the milk. The line formed slowly and stayed thin. A lot of the herdsmen did not come. And the ones who did come bought pink tickets as the girls from the dairy feared. The customs officers were the first ones there. They bought white tickets. I saw right away that the head officer was not in the line. Massi didn't say anything. Officer Fred explained why the head officer wasn't there. This is the first time he has not come to the dancehall. He got his evaluation, and it is worse than ever. His evaluation is bad because he closes down his customs office on Saturday nights. That forces the traffic into the other valleys. It is bad for the reputation of his office, it's a sign of slackness. If he keeps on getting such bad evaluations, the head customs officer will never be named to a more important office, and he might even lose the title of head officer, which he got by seniority after a lot of hard work. Officer Fred thinks the head officer is at an age when he should be thinking of his career. He has thought about the dancehall long enough. He let himself get carried away. The dancehall came before the customs office. It couldn't go on that way. The head customs officer wants to straighten himself out, and he decided to reopen the customs office on Saturday nights. He wants to show that he is not done for. He refuses to listen to the herdsmen who blame him for the sickness affecting the herds. Massi is out of luck. Her relationship with the head customs officer has barely begun, and already he has given up on the dancehall. She has lost her best and most faithful customer. It didn't do any good to go down to the valley below every day. I will not miss the head customs officer. Massi will be able to take care of officer Ted. Two officers is enough.

It was too much to hope that Massi would take care of officer Ted. She asked the girls from the dairy to take over at the gramophone, and she went up to her room. If she liked the dancehall as much as she says, she would not go and relax in her room on a Saturday night. Just because the head customs officer is not there, that doesn't mean she should neglect the other officers. She is depending entirely on me. There is no atmosphere in the main room. The girls from the dairy are doing all they can to tempt the herdsmen, and to make them buy blue tickets. The blue tickets bring in a lot more than the pink tickets. But they are not having any luck. The herdsmen are worried, they don't feel like going up to the rooms. The atmosphere is not good. Officer Fred wanted to go upstairs right after the first dance, like last week. In my room, he gave me two white tickets like last Saturday. I didn't understand. After all, he had told me there would only be one time that he would give me two tickets, because there is only one time that it's the first time. And here he is giving me two tickets again. He explained that tonight it is because he wants to come up to my room twice, that's why he bought two tickets. He will come up again when I have finished with officer Ted and the probationary officer. He said he was so pleased last Saturday that he wanted to go upstairs twice this Saturday. I make a change from Massi. He likes my style. Massi always wore straight slit sateen dresses, and he prefers organdy dresses with flounces. Since officer Fred is quick, it doesn't bother me that he bought two tickets. I will earn as much tonight as last Saturday, I will have at least four white tickets. This time with officer Fred, it didn't hurt, and there was no blood. I have a better idea of how to go about it. You soon learn how to go about it with a customs officer. It's easy with officer Fred, since he is quick and easy to please. Afterwards, I danced with officer Ted. Even though there was no atmosphere, he wanted to dance as long as last week. I was almost as tired, but I didn't sweat as much since it was not as hot. I was afraid he had bought two white tickets as well. I would not have been able to dance so long twice with officer Ted. But he only bought one ticket. He knows how to get full value from it. This time I didn't look in the mirror to see what officer Ted was doing. It's exactly like last time in the mirror. I have already seen everything once, I don't feel like seeing everything twice. I thought about Massi again. She has known a lot of customs officers. Now she must want to rest, since I am there to replace her. She overestimated the head officer. She places so much importance on titles because she used to be the wife of the mayor and school-teacher of Forever Valley. What she really wanted was to attract the mayor and the schoolteacher of the valley below to her dancehall. That would have been proof of her success. It was a blow for her that they never came up to Forever Valley. So she focused her attention on the head customs officer. She wanted to devote herself entirely to him. She could not have foreseen that he would prefer his career. Now he has made his choice between the dancehall and the customs office. Massi no longer wants to deal with ordinary customs officers, that would make her feel like she was slipping. She should not have changed her hair color. She doesn't want to fall to the level of the girls from the dairy, after all. The herdsmen are not for me, and they are not for her either. When he is enjoying his white ticket, officer Ted isn't concerned with what I am thinking about. As long as he can do whatever he likes, he is happy.

The probationary customs officer didn't look any better than he did last week. He wanted to dance anyway, to show me that he remembered what I had taught him. But before long he got dizzy, and I made him stop dancing in the middle of a dance. All we need now is for him to lose consciousness in front of the herdsmen, this is not the night for that. He followed me to my room. He gave me his white ticket right away. But he still didn't tell me his name, probably because he was feeling unwell. He had just lain down on the bed when suddenly he felt faint. But he didn't lose consciousness. I thought it was asthma, because he was having trouble breathing. But he told me it was his heart. He has a heart lesion. He says he can live with it. He doesn't understand why he has been having so many attacks since he was appointed probationary officer at the customs office. He never had attacks before. Now his attacks come on when he is alone at the customs office, or when he is at the dancehall. Again this Saturday, he won't get any good out of his white ticket. We had to wait while his attack subsided. When it was over, it was time for me to take care of officer Fred again. I don't know how to go about things with the probationary officer to keep him from feeling faint. Maybe I am going about it the wrong way. Massi never explained what to do in situations like this. Her door is closed. I can't go and disturb her. It is as if she weren't here tonight. The probationary officer said nothing when I asked him to go back downstairs. He is too happy that I haven't told anyone about his attacks. He doesn't want anyone to know he has a lesion. A customs officer has to have a solid heart. He is grateful to me for keeping his secret. Officer Fred was just as pleased the second time as the first. Officer Ted is cleverer. He takes longer with just one ticket than officer Fred does with two. They do not have the same temperament. It's a good thing for me that all the customs officers are not like officer Ted. I never forget to wash myself like Massi taught me.

The dancehall closed earlier tonight. The herdsmen were in a hurry to go back down to the valley. The girls from the dairy were dejected. This was really a bad Saturday for them, maybe the worst. They gave me a mean look as they were leaving. Right away they saw the four white tickets I was holding in my hand. They must be thinking their luck was really against them. I went and knocked on Massi's door. She was sitting in her armchair. She had taken off her straight slit sateen dress. She gave me the money she owed me in exchange for my tickets. On the dresser there is a picture of her husband, the former mayor of Forever Valley. He is dressed like a schoolteacher. I never noticed that photo before. I still said nothing to Massi about the probationary officer. I didn't feel like staying in her room. She didn't keep me. I am as tired as I was last Saturday. The dancehall is much more tiring than the pit. Massi asked me to turn out the lights and lock the door. I am the one who does everything at the dancehall now. Massi only had one night to devote to the head customs officer. He made full use of the dancehall. Now he can think about his career. Massi must be wondering about the future of her relationship with the head officer.

§6

I really earned my second Sunday. I am recuperating. I need it so I can see my project through. The father can say he is helping me, but I know this is a one-person project. Too bad for the father if he feels bored on Sundays. He can always read his book. But he has put it away in the drawer. He is not interested in reading anymore. He misses the pit on Sundays. He can no longer go into the garden alone. So he wheels himself through the rectory. He says his wheelchair rolls easily on the tile floor. He is forgetting that the wheels squeak, and that it bothers me when I am trying to rest. I don't know why the father can't stay in one place anymore. He must need to move all the time so he can forget that his legs are paralyzed. The only time he stops moving is when he is by the edge of the pit. As soon as I got back from the dancehall, I gave him the money I had earned. I thought that would calm him down. Last Sunday, that kept him calm all day long. This time, he put it in his drawer without any reaction. He seems detached from everything, even from the money I earn at the dancehall. You would think his paralysis was completely changing his way of seeing things. For the first time, he locked the drawer. He is becoming suspicious. He doesn't want me to open the drawer and go through his things. He must think the dancehall might be giving me ideas I never had before. He looks at me warily. When he was done rolling his wheelchair this way and that, he stopped in front of his harmonium and began to play. I am constantly being tormented by the father's noise. The harmonium sounded bad enough before, but now it is worse because it's going out of tune. I understand why I have been playing so many wrong notes lately. The songs I was playing badly, the father plays as badly as I did. So it comes from the harmonium. The father must not have much of an ear if he can go on playing like that. He doesn't appreciate the fact that I spend Sundays resting in my room instead of looking for the dead. He says no one my age ever needs to recuperate. You can see he has never been to the dancehall. I am not in my normal state on Sundays.

It took me a while to decide where to dig the second pit. The father wanted me to dig it right next to the first one, but I didn't listen to him. I would rather dig somewhere other than behind the church, since I found nothing behind the church. I am going to dig on the east, beside the church, on the opposite side from the rectory, so the second pit won't be visible either. You never know. What if Massi decided all of a sudden she wanted to look out at the garden when she comes to the rectory? I don't want her to find out. She doesn't usually look out at the garden. She only likes rock, and until now the garden was the only place in Forever Valley where there were no rocks. Forever Valley has a desolate landscape. Massi says it has a certain grandeur. I only like the rectory garden myself. The pits make me forget that the church is falling to pieces. Something must be done to keep the walls from collapsing. I can't look for the dead and take care of having the church walls reinforced at the same time. The father sees nothing but the pits. I never go for walks behind the hamlet, I don't like the mountains where nothing grows. There is nothing but rock. You have to have a real taste for it to take the path that leads up to the pass. Massi can say that the landscape of Forever Valley has a certain grandeur, but she doesn't go for walks behind the hamlet any more than I do. She lives closed up in her dancehall, except for last week when she went down to the valley below, but that was an exception. Of course, she has a view of the mountains and the rock from the dancehall. She can admire them at her leisure. She is not going to take an interest in the rectory garden all of a sudden. People's tastes don't change at her age. The father approved when I told him I was going to dig the second pit on the east. He said that was the direction of the sunrise. He seems pleased that I chose that side. He sees signs everywhere in the sky now that he has stopped reading his book.

On Monday, the father comes back to life. I had a hard time pushing his wheelchair into the garden. It's not working properly. The father forced it while he was wheeling himself through the rectory. Massi says it's a very advanced model, but what good does that do if it doesn't work? I have discovered a better technique for digging. The father says I am making progress. The second pit took shape very quickly. This time I laid out a bigger rectangle than for the first one. The bigger the pit, the more chance I have of finding the dead. The father had a surprise for me. He bought me some tonic. He secretly ordered it from a traveling salesman. The father says the tonic will help me grow. I took the tonic to keep him happy. It has a bitter taste. I have nothing against tonic. Maybe it will be good for my development. The father gets everything mixed up. It's not my growth that is slow, but my development. Maybe my muscles won't get so sore if I take tonic. For himself, the father bought some sedatives so his back pains won't torture him so. Sitting in his wheelchair all the time, even propped up with all his pillows, gives him unbearable back pains. Massages have no effect, sedatives are the only thing that helps. The father's pains go away when he is lying down. But he doesn't want to stay in bed while I am looking for the dead. So he really has to take his sedatives. In the end, the sedatives are a good idea. But they also cause problems. As you would expect, they make him drowsy. Sometimes there is nothing he can do about it, the father drifts off. When he wakes up, he is unhappy about having drifted off, and his day is spoiled. He is almost always in a bad mood now, because of the sedatives. And yet he can't do without them, or his back pains would become a real torture. I know how he feels. Digging like I am digging also causes back pains. But I know they are only temporary pains, and they will go away as I build myself up. Whereas with the father it is the opposite, he knows his pains are only going to get worse. His morale isn't good, even when he is sitting by the pit. To make things worse, I am still not finding anything, even though I am digging the second pit faster than the first. I am not discouraged. Ever since I started thinking about my project, I have accepted the idea that looking for the dead will take time. The father doesn't see things the way I do. He cannot take the sun. Even with his hat, he is uncomfortable. I tried to persuade him to stay inside the rectory during the hottest part of the day. But he is stubborn. He doesn't want me to be the first one to find the dead. He is getting too much sun. I can't dig with a clear mind because of the father. The main problem is still the church. There are stones falling into the pit I am digging. I have to take them out. That adds to the work. I got tired of seeing all the stones lying in the garden. I piled them up in the church. I don't like to look at the pile. The church doesn't look like anything at all anymore.

Massi came a day late to bring her money to the father. On Monday, I went to see what was the matter with her. I have been worried about the dancehall ever since I found out the herds are sick. It is the herdsmen that keep the dancehall going, not the customs officers. If the herdsmen have no more money to spend, that will be the end of the dancehall. Massi had not even cleaned up the main room, or the bedrooms either. Everything is just as messy as when I locked up the dancehall in the early morning. Massi is still in her room. She seems tired. The head customs officer asked her not to come down to the valley below. It would look even worse to the herdsmen if they found out that Massi was coming to see him every day. They would say he wasn't doing his job and wasn't checking anything. The head officer wants to be beyond reproach. Massi is right to be worried. This tension between the herdsmen and the customs office is not good for the dancehall. The dancehall needs both, herdsmen and customs officers. Massi gave me the father's treat. It's another of the cakes she bought last week in the valley below. She could not go on forever making a cake for the father every morning. The father said the cake was stale and didn't melt in his mouth. When Massi came to see him the next day, he did not even notice that she was looking unwell. He took her money without counting it or even noticing how little there was of it. When he saw that all Massi had to give him was her money, he asked for his cake. Until now, Massi has always given him his treat along with the money. The father said the cake was even more stale than the day before, and he didn't want any. Massi looked like someone who had been caught red-handed. She asked the father to forgive her because the herds in the valley below were sick and the herdsmen were suspicious of the customs office, and that was bad for the dancehall. She must have hoped the father would understand and forgive her for the treat. But he gave her an angry look as if he didn't understand at all. He did not even explain to her how he was going to invest her money. Massi didn't dare ask any questions. I am afraid the father will not put up with being deprived of his treat. He doesn't seem to care at all about the future of the dancehall. He put the money in the drawer and locked the drawer.

Massi has not come back to see the father, and the father hasn't said anything about Massi. I go to see Massi every evening, after I spend all day digging the second pit. Massi lives closed up in her room. Her gramophone is always playing. Everything is in a mess. The lights are on even in broad daylight. She is going to wear out her generator, running it the way she does. She is wasting light. I tried on a straight slit sateen dress to see how it looked on me. It doesn't suit me at all. I am not big enough. I don't seem to have any shape at all in a straight slit sateen dress. Massi showed me how to wash my organdy dresses. I can't buy a new dress every Saturday. I have to learn how to look after my dresses myself. I also learned how to iron the flounces. Since I am not used to ironing, I made creases. My dresses are not so pretty now that they have been washed and ironed. They have creases and folds, and they have lost their sizing. Massi says she is like a girl from the dairy who has grown too old to work at the dancehall. And what a strange idea it was to dye her hair that color. She says she understands the head customs officer's decision. A customs officer has to think of his career first. The dancehall was not good for the head officer. He would already have been named to a more important office if he had not always been at the dancehall with his men. Massi drew the customs officers into the dancehall, and now she is disparaging the dancehall. She says the dancehall was a bad influence on the customs officers. She also says she has never gotten over being widowed. No customs officer, not even the head officer, was ever able to make her forget that she was once the wife of the mayor and schoolteacher of

Forever Valley. She is forgetting that the dancehall was a new lease on life for her. She says she misses the days when there was no customs office. She almost agrees with the girls from the dairy that the customs office is bad for the valley below. I don't understand why she is saying all that. She says she is going to use the fruit of her investments to build a beautiful brand-new dancehall in the valley below, just for the herdsmen. She is going to go deaf with the gramophone on so loud all day long. I told the father Massi wasn't doing well. He told me he wasn't doing well either. His paralysis is spreading, as he feared. The father and Massi are both having difficulties at the same time.

The second pit still hasn't produced anything. I ran into another layer of soil all of a sudden. It's heavy and sticky, and hard to handle with the shovel. It looks like mud. I still have not found the dead. The father must have increased his dosage of sedatives, because he drifts off more and more often. He leaves me alone to dig. I don't know where the dead are. That doesn't keep me from looking. I am looking blindly. The father has lost weight since he stopped having his treats. It's bad for him to lose weight, it saps his strength. He can't keep himself upright anymore. I try to think about the dead as I dig, but it is hard to think and dig at the same time. The shovel gets heavier and heavier, because the soil is like mud. The second pit looks different from the first one. Massi says the dancehall is doing me good and that I am looking well. She doesn't know I am taking tonic. She knows nothing about my activities. She thinks I live only for the dancehall. Maybe she thinks I will be able to replace her completely. She seemed so well two weeks ago. Maybe her fatigue was already starting then. I couldn't see it because I was ignorant. I have learned a great deal in two weeks. I can't count on Massi or the father. Massi is not a model like the father always said she was. And the father is just the opposite of what he says.

§7

The third Saturday, I was almost as nervous as the first Saturday. I wonder how the situation has developed in the valley below. During the week, I live cut off from everything. It's not good that the valley below is completely dependent on milk for its livelihood. All it takes is one sickness in the herds to ruin everything. I hope Massi has cleaned up the dancehall. Even if she approves of the head customs officer's decision, it still did something to her to learn that he would never come back to the dancehall. Her dream was that there would be nothing but customs officers at the dancehall. She had to accept the herdsmen, because the customs office was too small to keep the dancehall going. The father is always gloomy on Saturday mornings. Instead of enjoying his time in front of the pit, he is already thinking about what is coming up, a long day and a half languishing all alone in the rectory. He used to say there was nothing better than the coolness of the rec-

tory in the summertime. And now he is miserable whenever he is in the rectory. The sedatives have no effect on his
misery. They are only good for the pains in his back. I don't know why the father should be miserable in his own rectory. Maybe it's knowing that starting at noon on Saturdays my mind is not on the dead but on the dancehall. The dancehall is foreign to him now that he has lost interest in the money I earn. I would miss the dancehall if I never went there again. It breaks things up for me. After all, I can't look for the dead seven days a week. It would end up going to my head. That's what is happening to the father. The dead are going to his head. And to make things worse, I never found anything in the second pit. I had to give up on it. I couldn't dig in that mud anymore. It had turned into a kind of sludge. My hands and feet were black when I came in from the pit. I had a hard time washing it off. There is no real bathroom in the rectory, everything is very rudimentary, just a faucet and a basin. I told the father I was running into difficulties as insurmountable as in the first pit. In the first one it was rock, and in the second it's sludge. The father had to resign himself to this second defeat. I could not even clean the sludge off the shovel. It was disgusting to dig in those conditions. The father thinks it must be the underground spring that is producing the sludge. There is no point in looking for the dead in the direction of the sunrise. The dead are not in the sludge. On the other hand, the sludge does attract insects. The second pit is already infested with insects. The garden

surprises you when you dig in it. On the surface, it looks the same everywhere, but the surface is deceptive. You would never know there was rock on the north and sludge on the east. The father will have all weekend to think about his disappointment. That is not going to do him any good. He stuffed himself with sedatives. I finished my tonic.

I didn't make good use of my Saturday afternoon. I could not stop thinking about the dancehall. I got there early. I was relieved. Massi had straightened everything up. All the same, it has been two weeks since she waxed the floor. With all the lights on, you can see every scratch. My flounces are not as crisp as last Saturday. That's because the dress was washed and ironed. Organdy does not stand up to washing like sateen, it's easily damaged. Massi has a new dress, but she is looking her age. She is sitting on a chair, waiting for the dancehall to open. The girls from the dairy came on time. They are not yellow anymore, but their faces are covered with brown spots. You can't call it an improvement. This week they had almost no work at all at the dairy. The herds are no longer giving milk. The girls from the dairy say the milk fever didn't exist before the customs office opened up. I can understand why they always say bad things about the customs office. They have always been looked down on by the customs officers. If the customs office weren't there, their pride would never be wounded. They were happy to be able to tell Massi that the herdsmen had put pressure on the mayor to close the customs office. There are already plenty of offices in the other valleys. The other valleys are not used for raising livestock. They are better suited to the traffic created by the border. Massi said nothing. She must be weighing both sides of the argument. She doesn't know what to think yet. The girls told Massi the brown spots on their faces were a sign that the liver disease was running its course and that it would not be long before their skin became white again. They are trying to reassure Massi. I wonder how spots like that are going to just disappear. When the skin is pigmented, it stays that way. The girls from the dairy hope that lots of herdsmen will come to the dancehall tonight to forget their cares. They have faith in the mayor. The mayor wants only the best for the valley below. The girls from the dairy hope it will be a good Saturday, one of the best. They are wearing a lot of perfume. They have put on a darker shade of makeup to hide the brown spots. No matter what they do, they still have no style. If the customs office closes, I will lose my position at the dancehall. There is no way I will ever do the same work as the girls from the dairy. Besides, my style doesn't please the herdsmen. I am made for the customs officers. Maybe it's not a coincidence that Massi changed her style. But no matter what she does, the herdsmen will never mistake her for a girl from the dairy.

The girls from the dairy knew what they were talking about. The line formed at the usual time. All the herdsmen were in a hurry to get in. They all bought green tick-ets. Tonight, they all want to do some dancing and then go up to the rooms. The girls from the dairy will not have a moment's rest with all the green tickets that were sold. I would not agree to work at the dancehall in conditions like that. The herdsmen are so happy to dance that they don't even notice the unwaxed dance floor. Massi is in charge of the gramophone. She is not shutting herself in her room tonight. She is on the dance floor. She is dancing with the herdsmen for the first time. I was unpleasantly surprised to see that neither officer Fred nor officer Ted was in the line. The probationary officer was the only one in the line. I will only get one white ticket tonight. The probationary officer is looking a little better. He told me officers Fred and Ted were also working at the customs office tonight, with the head officer. Only the probation-ary officer had the right to go to the dancehall, because he is not a real customs officer yet. With all the threats hang-ing over the office, the head customs officer has taken steps. He wants all his officers to be beyond reproach like him, so he can say in his report that the officers are on the job even on Saturday nights. It's always bad for a customs officer to go to a dancehall. He might let himself get car-ried away. And then he can make mistakes in his work. The head customs officer hopes to get a better evaluation, and he also hopes to prevent the closing of the customs office. There is no contact between the herdsmen and the customs officers anymore. The customs officers want traf-

fic, and the herdsmen are against traffic. They can't get
along. The probationary officer is not wearing his customs
officer's uniform. He doesn't want to be noticed. He is
afraid. He wouldn't know how to strike back if the herdsmen went after him. But the herdsmen are not interested
in going after a probationary officer. A probationary officer is not a customs officer yet. The herdsmen are sure of
themselves tonight. They see it as a victory that the customs officers have stopped coming up to the dancehall.
From now on, they are the masters. Massi must be trying
to flatter the herdsmen by dancing with them. She did not
even look at the probationary customs officer. He doesn't
seem at ease all alone at the dancehall. Still, he looks better
in his street clothes. He looks nothing like a customs officer. But you can see he is not a herdsman. You can't tell
what he is. He must have come to the dancehall so the
other customs officers wouldn't think he was afraid of
coming all alone. I don't know if he wants to become a
customs officer, but he is afraid of being judged unworthy
of it.

I was nice to the probationary customs officer. He danced
better tonight. We danced every other dance. I want to
look after him. Now that I know he has a lesion, I don't
want to wear out his heart. He gets out of breath easily. It's
a good thing he came. Otherwise what would I have done?
Massi would surely have sent me back to the rectory. She
would not want me standing around like a wallflower all

night at the dancehall. I would rather be a wallflower than dance with a herdsman. I am not like Massi. With her new style, the herdsmen like her, for dancing at least. When I saw that the probationary customs officer was really getting out of breath, I suggested we go up to my room. He seems to like it when I make the suggestion. He doesn't dare ask on his own. As soon as he got to the room, he gave me his white ticket. And then he told me his name. He is called Bob. Bob is a much better name than Fred or Ted. All customs officers are named Fred or Ted. This time he wanted to get some good out of his white ticket. But he couldn't manage to catch his breath. I realized right away that he would not be able to manage. I should not have made him dance so long. Even dancing just every other dance, he lost his breath. He doesn't feel faint tonight. And yet he still can't get any good out of his white ticket. He can say he has learned to live with his lesion, but it is still a handicap. He can't live a normal life. I am not sure he is cut out to be a customs officer. High altitudes are bad for the heart. I did everything I could to take care of him. I don't want him to stop coming to the dancehall. He stayed in my room for a long time. He is all I have to keep me busy tonight. It took him quite a while to catch his breath, much longer than officer Ted takes with his white ticket. It doesn't bother me that he is not getting any good out of his white ticket. It only bothers me for his sake. I would not want him to be cheated. White tickets are expensive, especially for a probationary officer. He seemed pleased all the same. The customs officers will think he got plenty of good out of his white ticket, and they will regret not being probationary officers anymore.

The dancehall closed late. The girls from the dairy were triumphant with their green tickets, especially when they saw that I only had one white ticket. I don't miss officers Fred and Ted. I am not tired at all. But just looking at their faces, you can tell the girls from the dairy will have a hard time recuperating, especially since they are going to have to go back to work at the dairy. Massi looks tired, too. Dancing with the herdsmen is tiring. All night long, she never even went up to rest in her room. She didn't give me anything in exchange for my white ticket. She said I owed her for two organdy dresses with flounces and a pair of patent leather heels, and that came to just what the ticket costs. I had forgotten I still owed her. There is nothing I can say. Massi's figures are right. She still has a head for business. I earned nothing tonight. What good would the money do me anyway? The father keeps it in his drawer, and I don't even have a key to the drawer. Massi is thinking about the future of the dancehall of Forever Valley. Her relationship with the head customs officer is already finished. It was not a real relationship like she hoped. The customs officers will not come to the dancehall again. Massi must be wondering if I am worth keeping just for the probationary officer. There is nothing but the herdsmen now.

§8

The father woke up when he heard me come in. He put out his hand so I could give him the money I had earned at the dancehall. But when he saw that his hand was still empty, he put it back down without saying anything. Putting his hand out was an automatic gesture. He didn't even ask me why I had not earned anything at the dancehall. It's a bad sign that the father has become so indifferent. He says he is not feeling well. The sedatives are interfering with his sleep. He has bad dreams. He dreams about the dead, and they are bad dreams. It was spending the night alone in the rectory that put him in this state. I can't count on the dancehall anymore. My position is in danger, I can feel it, even if Massi has said nothing to me. My project has not gone anywhere. I have dug two pits, but they are empty pits. Time is moving faster all of a sudden. I wasn't ready for it. In the rectory, my life was always quiet and well-ordered. I feel all shaken up inside. I was used to officers Fred and Ted. And now I have nothing left but Bob. I have nothing to feel guilty about. It is not my fault they have stopped coming. It's because the head customs officer started thinking of his career all of a sudden, after all this time thinking of nothing but the dancehall. The father showed me his fingers. He can't move them anymore. He says his paralysis is spreading to his upper limbs. He seems unhappy. He feels alone. He dreams of the dead too often. He is terrified at night.

I spent all Sunday in my room without any disturbances from the father. I am not tired, but I need to be alone to think about the dead. The father is no longer strong enough to get around the rectory in his wheelchair, or maybe he just doesn't want to. As for the harmonium, he can't play it anymore now that his fingers are becoming paralyzed. He must finally have realized that the harmonium is out of tune. It must have such an ugly sound because it was never tuned properly. Where will I dig now? I have dug on the north side of the church, and I have dug on the east. I am going to dig on the south side, just in front of the door to the church. It's not really a door anymore. It wouldn't take anything at all to make it collapse. And the walls are not really walls anymore either. It's a sad thing to see the garden with the pile of rocks getting bigger every day and the church that is no longer a church. If I dig in front of the door to the church, the third pit will be visible from the rectory. What do I care if Massi sees the third pit? Without the customs officers, the dancehall isn't the dancehall anymore. I wanted to do something nice to thank the father for letting me spend all afternoon resting in my room without being bothered by his creaky wheelchair. I suggested we go for a walk in the garden. I know he likes to go for walks in the garden in the evening. He wanted to go and see the pits. He looked at the first pit for a long time. The pit looks clean and tidy thanks to the solid rock at the bottom. It looks like it was put there for a reason. The father said it was a beautiful pit. Next we stopped in front of the second pit. We could not stay long because of all the insects attracted by the sludge. I told the father it would be better if I filled this one in. It isn't pleas- ant to look at, and you can't stay near it for long because of the insects. The father said no, once a pit is dug, you have to leave it as it is. I don't know where he gets his rules. I do not agree with him. Nothing good is going to come from the sludge. But I can't disagree with the father about every- thing. I told him I would dig the third pit in front of the church starting tomorrow. He approved. He said that was a very good place, the place of honor for the dead. He said nothing as we passed by the pile of stones or the ruined church.

I got up early to prepare the ground for the third pit, and to lay out its placement very precisely. It will be a pit of exactly the same dimensions as the first pit. I want there to be symmetry between the front and the back of the church. I am not really digging at random after all, I am digging on each side of the church, at the four points of the compass. That is as good a plan as any other. It didn't occur to me at first, but now I see it clearly. The father is already up. He showed me his hands right away. They look as if they had turned to stone. I don't have as far to go to push the father's wheelchair over to the third pit. I got him settled in by the edge as usual. This is the third week I have been digging. I don't wear myself out with useless gestures anymore. Even though the father is becoming more and more paralyzed, he is still as lucid as ever. He pays attention to everything. His fear vanishes as soon as

he is in the garden by the edge of the pit. He is only afraid in the rectory because of his bad dreams. I am not finding anything in the third pit. Maybe the father is closer to the dead than I am, since he dreams about them. He never reads his book anymore, he dreams. But they are bad dreams. He decided to stop taking his sedatives, since his back pains are gone. I said nothing about it to him, but if his pains are gone, it might be because his paralysis has spread to his nerves. Nerves are what cause pain. Not taking his sedatives will clean out his system. Maybe he will stop having bad dreams. He has a hard time sitting upright in his wheelchair. He leans to one side and then to the other. He will end up with curvature of the spine that way. There is nothing that can be done about it.

I was amazed to see Massi come to the rectory at the usual time, as if everything were normal. She seems sure of herself. She made a cake for the father, his favorite kind. She must want to ask him for something since she is trying to get back into his good graces after what happened last week. She did not understand why the father didn't take his cake from her. I had to explain that the father's hands were paralyzed now. Massi does not realize how far the father's paralysis has progressed. She has not asked after him for a week. I noticed she didn't have with her the money she had taken in at the dancehall last time. And yet she took in a great deal of money, even without the customs officers. I was right to think she wanted to ask the father for something. She is clever. First she asked me to feed him his cake. The father took a big mouthful. But he couldn't swallow it. Massi waited for him to swallow. When she saw he still could not manage, she decided to speak. She asked the father to give her back all her investments. It must be for her project to build a brand-new dancehall in the valley below. Also, she must think the father is in no condition to make her money bear fruit anymore. I can understand why she would want to take back her money. The father could have given it to her without her having to ask, since he never thinks about it anymore. The father took his time answering. He still could not swallow his treat. When he finally managed to do it, it went down the wrong way. That was when Massi realized what a state the father was in. Maybe she didn't really want to know? She said we needed to let in some air so the father could breathe, and she opened the window herself. That was when she saw the third pit just in front of the door to the church. She did not expect to see the garden in such a state. She also saw the other two pits, since the church walls are not as high as they used to be. The air helped the father immediately. He finally managed to swallow the whole mouthful. He looked Massi right in the eye and told her I was looking for the dead and that was why I was digging pits in the rectory garden. He said it wasn't a garden like she thought, but a cemetery. Massi didn't say what was on her mind. She doesn't want any problems with the father right when she is trying to get her investments back. The father had a funny smile as Massi tried to control herself and asked him again for her investments. He took the key out of his pocket and asked me to go get the box from the drawer. Next he asked me to open the box. Then Massi could see all the money she had entrusted to the father so he could make it bear fruit. The money is arranged in little bundles, in order, one bundle for each week. The father never invested anything at all. He deceived Massi. All she had to do was ask for some sort of verification, instead of taking the father at his word. Why did she always take him at his word? All she has now is a little savings, instead of the tidy sum she thought she would get when her money bore fruit. She surely doesn't have enough savings to pay for the beautiful brand-new dancehall she was hoping to build in the valley below. She looks crushed. She would never have believed the father could deceive her that way. She did not even have enough strength to curse him. Besides, in his condition, the father is insensitive to everything, even curses. He must think he has nothing to feel guilty about. He took nothing from Massi. He just kept her money in his drawer instead of making it bear fruit. I didn't think the father knew anything about investments, but I would not have thought he wasn't investing anything at all. Massi let herself be taken in by the father. She was so overcome by the shock that she left without saying a word about the pits. But they had an effect on her. The father did not ask me to give him back the key to the drawer. I left it in the lock. The money I earned from the dancehall can't even be called savings. Massi has something, at least. I don't.

The father is not feeling well. He still wants to go with me to the pit. He would still rather be out in the sunshine watching me dig than stay in the rectory by himself. Day after day, I dig. The father has an empty stare. He has lost his appetite. He is getting thinner. I put stones from the church under the wheels of his wheelchair to keep it from rolling. The father can't move his wheelchair when it is blocked by stones. It's safer that way, since the brakes are defective. I dig without finding anything. I wonder where the dead are. Massi has not come back to see the father. She will never set foot in the rectory again now that she has seen the pits and the father has told her I was looking for the dead. I went to see her. She asked if it was the father's idea that I look for the dead. I told her it was my personal project but that the father approved of it. She said she would never have thought I was capable of that. She hired me at the dancehall in good faith and for my benefit. And I deceived her by hiding the fact that I had a personal project. She said she had been deceived by every-one, me, the customs officers, and the father. She says she is ruined. She is not ruined, since the father gave her back all the money she made from the dancehall. She doesn't know what she is saying anymore. She is getting everything mixed up, the dead, the investments, the dancehall. She can't bear to think of me looking for the dead right across from the dancehall. She says Forever Valley has become uninhabitable because of the pits I am digging in the rectory garden. I am not angry with her. It is not her fault that she doesn't understand anything about the dead.

I had to stop digging the third pit. The shovel ran into solid rock all of a sudden. It's exactly like in the first pit. It is the same rock. There is a huge ridge of rock running across the garden from north to south, deep down. There is rock everywhere in Forever Valley, even underneath the garden. You have to dig to find that out. When you dig in front of and behind the church, you find the ridge of rock. You do not find the dead.

§9

This is my fourth Saturday at the dancehall, but this is the first Saturday I have not had any digging to do. I am not going to begin digging the fourth pit on a Saturday morning. The father didn't want to go out, he wanted to stay in bed. That is a bad sign. He doesn't even seem to be afraid of staying by himself in the rectory anymore. I went for a walk in the garden without the father. The flowers are all blooming at once. The flowers smell good in the morning because of the evening dew. It was the father who made all the flowers grow in the garden, back when he still maintained it. Now the flowers grow all by themselves. Even though the garden is covered with flowers, it is a terrible mess. You wonder what those three pits are doing there, and that pile of stones getting bigger and bigger in the middle of the ruined church. I don't like the second pit. Sludge is not what you expect to see in Forever Valley. The father is wondering about the dead, he doesn't know what to think about them anymore. He says maybe I was wrong to try to look for the dead in his garden. He is forgetting that he encouraged me. He has misconceptions about the dead which torment him. He has lost movement in his arms. I don't know what to do for him anymore.

Saturday afternoon went by slowly. The rectory has never been so quiet. The father doesn't move at all in his bed. I went to the dancehall at the usual time. Massi had added a word on the sign that says dancing. I don't know what it means. There are times when not knowing how to read is an inconvenience. I went right up to see Massi. That was the first thing she told me, what it said on the sign. She had not forgotten that I don't know how to read. She told me that it said: closed. Massi is closing the dancehall. There will be no more Saturday nights at the dancehall of Forever Valley. Nothing is in its place inside. The floor has not shone since it was last polished three weeks ago. Massi was not wearing her straight slit sateen dress. She gave me a package. It was my two organdy dresses and my patent leather high heels. They are mine, since I paid her for them last Saturday. She had even washed and ironed the dresses. What will I do with them? They are not the thing to wear at the rectory. Massi says she can never open her dancehall again now that there is a cemetery facing it. She says it wouldn't be right. She believes what the father told her, that the rectory garden is a cemetery. Until I find the dead it is not a cemetery, it's still a garden. It's dark in the dancehall. The generator is out of order and there is no more electricity. The gramophone isn't working, and neither are the fans. Nothing works in the dancehall without the generator, since everything is electric. Massi seems resigned to it. She is not criticizing me for anything. I don't even know if she is angry with the father. In his condition, it's hard to be angry with him. She says I got the idea of looking for the dead because I was raised in the rectory. I would never have thought of it if I had been raised in the dancehall. I asked her what she was going to do now that the dancehall was closed. She wants to leave Forever Valley. She says she should have done it when her husband died, even then she knew it was unfit to live in. A hamlet without a town hall, without a school, and without a church isn't fit to live in. She thought the dancehall might make it fit to live in. She says she was mistaken. A hamlet that has lost everything cannot be kept alive by a dancehall alone. She says it is all because of the opening of the customs office. She hoped for too much from the customs officers. The customs officers disappointed her. She says she made a mistake. With her savings, she wants to build a little bungalow in the valley below. She has given up on the idea of building a dancehall just for the herdsmen. She doesn't have enough money, she is getting too old for it, and she is not the herdsmen's type. She wants to build her bungalow right near the cemetery where her husband, the mayor of Forever Valley, is buried. She feels guilty about letting his grave go downhill. She wants to have it redone and to care for it every day. She is trying to find a reason to live. She is not from the valley below, she is from Forever Valley. I can't hold her back.

When the girls from the dairy arrived, Massi let them in on her decision. She told them they could work for themselves on Saturday nights now that she had trained them. The herdsmen learned to appreciate them, they will remember the girls. But the girls from the dairy miss the dancehall already. To them, it's irreplaceable. They are not sure it will be so easy to work for themselves on Saturday nights, especially with those brown spots that they still have on their faces. The spots did not go away like they hoped. They are an indelible trace of the liver disease. Away from the dancehall the girls will lose their appeal, they know it and it torments them. They say Massi is closing the dancehall because of the customs officers. They think the customs officers brought them nothing but bad luck. They are bitter. The dairy is all they have left. They look faded already. The herdsmen came to the dancehall in great numbers. When they saw the sign, they turned around. They are happy, even if they came up here for nothing. It was a good week for them. They won out over the customs officers. The mayor of the valley below was authorized to shut down the customs office. The herdsmen hope the herds will be cured and the milk fever will disappear now that there will be no more traffic. The head customs officer did not lose out. The efforts he made to change his ways were repaid. He was just named head customs officer in a larger office. That is what he was hoping for. He will not miss the valley. He will forget about the dancehall. He is taking officers Fred and Ted with him. They were also promoted. Bob was the one who told me the news. He was hoping the dancehall would be open like every other Saturday. I thought he was looking well. He seemed disappointed when he saw what was written on the sign. Massi told me she wanted to spend the night alone in her closed dancehall. She sent me away like the others.

I stayed alone with Bob. He did not get any kind of promotion. He didn't have time to prove himself. The head customs officer had doubts about him at the last minute, and he wrote a bad report on him. Bob was not appointed customs officer. He isn't a probationary officer either, since he has reached the end of his probation. He isn't anything anymore. He doesn't know if he would have liked to be a customs officer like Fred or Ted. He says he might not be cut out for it, because of his lesion. Bob is not like anyone I know. Of course, apart from the father and Massi, I have never known anyone but officers Fred and Ted. I have always lived in the rectory with the father. Bob is out of work now that the customs office is closing and he is not a probationary officer anymore. He doesn't know where to go. He says he has nowhere to go. The father isn't much of a companion for me in the state he is in. And if Massi goes away, I will be all alone in the hamlet. If Bob wants to come and live in the rectory, there is room for him. He accepted right away. He prefers Forever Valley to the valley below, because there is no traffic. He could never have been a customs officer. All customs officers like traffic. I understand Bob. He's like me.

We came back to the rectory since the dancehall was closed. The father did not wake up. I showed Bob to his room. It's primitive, but Bob is used to that. At his age and in his condition, the father needs an assistant. Even if there is no more church, there is still a rectory at Forever Valley. I showed Bob around the garden. It's nice that there is a full moon. You can see almost as well as in daylight. Bob was surprised to discover the garden. You can't see it from the dancehall. He saw the pits as well. I told him I was looking for the dead. I don't want to keep anything from him. He looked at me without understanding. I tried to explain it to him. I must not have explained it very well, since he still did not understand after my explanations. I put on my organdy dress with flounces since it is Saturday night after all, even if the dancehall is closed. My dress is a little wrinkled. Massi must have creased it when she put it in the package she gave me before sending me away. I also put on my patent leather high heels, even though they are not very practical for walking in the garden. Bob has always seen me in my organdy dress and my patent leather shoes. I don't want him to think I have changed just because we are in the rectory instead of the dancehall. My dress is a little tight in the neckline. The water Massi washed it in must have been too hot, and it shrank. I am still not developed. The tonic had no effect. I don't mind. Still, Massi says sixteen is the right age. I told Bob I was sixteen and I was not developed. He didn't think there was anything wrong with that. That's good. He asked me if I was planning to go back to work in another dancehall. He told me he would go and dance in that dancehall. That was nice of him. I know he doesn't like to dance because of his heart. I told him no. I want to stay in Forever Valley. I don't like the valley below. Bob seemed relieved that I did not want to go back to work in some other dancehall. Deep down, he doesn't like the dancehall.

We spent the night by the edge of the third pit. It is the nicest pit because it's right in front of the church and it has a view of the mountains of Forever Valley. The flowers make a kind of white carpet. Bob said it was a beautiful garden. Bob and I have the same tastes. Even if he doesn't understand about the dead, what does that matter, since he likes the rectory garden as it is? We were both bitten by insects. That's the trouble with the second pit, it attracts insects that swarm as far away as the edge of the third pit. At night, the third pit looks deeper than it is. You can't see the rock at the bottom. I am very happy the dancehall is closed tonight and that Bob is here. I will never get any more white tickets. What does that matter? This Saturday night is not a Saturday night like the others. This is my first Saturday night with Bob away from the dancehall. Bob and I slept by the edge of the third pit. It had a lovely smell of flowers. The daylight woke us up.

§10

When the father woke up, I introduced Bob to him. I told him Bob was his assistant. Bob used to be a probationary customs officer, so he is perfectly able to become the father's assistant. The father looked at Bob without speaking. He could have said something to welcome him. After all, he has always dreamt of having an assistant. I understood all of a sudden why the father was not saying anything. The paralysis had spread to the lower half of his face. The father can no longer speak. This spreading paralysis would be a real torment for the father except that it has eased his pain. The father isn't suffering anymore. I understood from his expression that he was tired of lying down, and that he wanted me to put him in his wheelchair. That would not be wise in his condition, he might fall out. I strapped him to his wheelchair. Today is Sunday, I will not look for the dead. This is my day off, even though I am not working at the dancehall anymore. I took the father for a walk in the garden so he could get some fresh air. He closed his eyes. He didn't even open them when he was in front of the pits. It is as if he no longer wanted to see. When the walk was over, he was worn out. I put him back to bed.

Since it was Sunday, I showed Bob around Forever Valley. All he knows is the dancehall and the rectory. I have to show him the mountains as well. Massi always said the far end of Forever Valley is an undiscovered beauty spot. Her husband wanted to make it famous. He died without having succeeded. Bob agreed with Massi. He thought Forever Valley's setting had a certain grandeur. He noticed right away that the rock you see on the mountains is the same rock as at the bottom of the third pit. I don't like this place. It's too rugged, there is nothing but solid rock, loose stones, and dirt. Bob asked me where the path that goes up the steepest slope leads to. I told him what I had always been told, that it was the path that leads to the pass. The border is up there too. But there is no customs office in Forever Valley, it's too rugged for traffic. The customs office was opened in the valley below because it is much wider down there. I could see Bob was interested in what I was saying. He was not a probationary customs officer for nothing. Borders attract him, even ones without customs offices. They don't attract me. I have never been over the border. And yet it was easy to cross over in the valley be-

low, all you had to do was show your passport to the customs officer and he would open the border. I have never
had a passport. The father always said they were useless.
Massi has never been over the border either, even though
she spent so much time with customs officers. Bob wanted
to spend the afternoon there at the far end of Forever
Valley. I did it to make him happy. The mountains
changed colors with the sun. Bob said it made a lovely
spectacle. I don't like the place, but I agreed it made a
lovely spectacle and that it was worth it to spend Sunday
afternoon there because of the light on the mountains,
and then also because Bob was there with me. I would
never have stayed if I had been alone. Bob kept looking
towards the pass. There is a sort of notch in the mountain
where the path goes through. The pass is up there where
the mountain makes a kind of hole. You can see it clearly. I
had never looked at it before.

On Monday I started looking for the dead again. This is
my last chance. If I can't find the dead in the fourth pit,
then they are not in the rectory garden and I was wrong. I
put the father in front of the place where the fourth pit will
be, and I carefully laid out the perimeter like I learned to
do digging the other pits. The fourth pit has exactly the
same dimensions as the second. The symmetry of the pits
has to be maintained. The fourth pit faces west. The four
pits are laid out around the church. Strapped to his wheelchair, the father is in no danger of falling out. He keeps his

eyes closed. He doesn't even open them to watch me dig. Maybe that shows he is no longer interested in the dead, or else he has lost hope. But he has to stay by the edge of the fourth pit until I am done digging. That has always been his wish, and I want to respect his wishes until the end of the last pit. I can't be sure his mind is still working. The paralysis might have started spreading to his head already. The father is there by the edge of the fourth pit anyway, even if he closes his eyes. It is easy for me to dig now. I have been digging for four weeks, so I am in shape. I don't have any trouble lifting the shovel anymore. This time I even have an assistant. Bob digs with the pick. But he is clumsy, he has never used a pick before. He hit himself with the handle. He still wants to help me, even if he doesn't understand why I am digging. I don't want him to wear out his heart. I don't think I will find the dead in the direction of the sunset. That is not a good direction for the dead to face.

Massi packed all her belongings into crates. And then a truck came. I would never have thought such a big truck could have climbed the gravel road from the valley below all the way to Forever Valley. Massi completely emptied out the dancehall. She doesn't want to keep any of its furnishings. She is going to sell it all at auction. That was just what the father did with the property of the church. Now it is the dancehall's turn. It will be the most beautiful auction the valley below has ever seen. Massi had nothing but beautiful things in her dancehall, and her appliances were the latest and most advanced models. But her appliances are all electric, and there is no generator in the valley be- low. I wonder who would want to buy Massi's beautiful appliances. The herdsmen from the valley below have never seen the need for electricity. The valley below still has an old-fashioned way of life. Massi has always been ahead of her time. She thought the customs office and all the traffic it brought in would finally modernize the valley below. Now that the customs office is closed and there is no more traffic, I don't see what could force the valley below to modernize like Massi wants. She only likes modern things. The truck was packed full when it left. Massi left with the truck. She wants to make an abrupt break with the past. She is leaving the empty dancehall behind her. She took down the sign that said dancing. I have nothing left to read. There is nothing left but the words painted on the front of the house, town hall and school, or school and town hall, I don't know what order they are written in. Massi came to say goodbye to the father. She is not even angry with him anymore for not investing her money. She is not bitter. I don't know if the father recognized her, or if he understood that she was leaving Forever Valley. I don't think he is aware of anything anymore. That may be the best thing for him. He was very attached to Massi before he tried to find the dead. It did something to Massi to see what a state the father is in. She said it was a good thing he has an assistant. She looked at Bob for the first time. She told me she was happy I wouldn't be staying all alone with the father. She gave me her address so I could go see her in the valley below. While she is waiting for her bungalow to be finished, she will be living in the rest home. She noticed how startled I was to hear that word. She should not have said it in front of the father. Massi says the father was always prejudiced against the home. She doesn't know why, since it is the prettiest building in the valley below, the only one with all the conveniences, except electricity of course. And it is well located, near the church and the cemetery, across from the dairy. Massi wants to oversee the construction of her bungalow herself, and the home is near the lot she chose to build on. Since there are no hotels in the valley below, there are guest rooms at the home. Massi wanted me to stop worrying. She told me her bungalow would be finished very quickly. Nothing takes less time to put up than a bungalow. You don't even need to dig foundations, and it almost builds itself. Massi seems to know all about bungalows. No matter how impressive her house in Forever Valley was, Massi always thought it was too old, and yet she did everything she could to modernize it. But it was only putting new things into an old thing. And Massi wants nothing but new things. I don't understand why she would want to leave such a well-appointed house. She could at least have gone on living there until her bungalow is finished, instead of going and living in the home. But she wants to leave Forever Valley now. It seems strange to see someone her age abandon everything like that. She told me to look after the father. It does something to her to leave him, she has always known him. It must also do something to her to leave Forever Valley and the dancehall, but she didn't show it. She told me that when the truck reached the entrance to the gravel road that leads up to Forever Valley from the valley below, she would get out and take down the sign pointing the way to the dancehall. There is no more dancehall in Forever Valley. There is nothing but an abandoned former town hall and former school. Bob does not feel concerned about Massi's departure or about the closing of the dancehall. He has never lived in Forever Valley. It means nothing to him. He can't understand the way I do. Massi has always lived across from the rectory. She should not have left. Now there is nothing but the rectory in Forever Valley.

Whenever he has time, Bob takes a walk behind the hamlet, in the mountains. He likes the landscape. He spends hours walking on the path that leads to the pass. I can't go with him. I have to look after the father. The father is not doing well at all. His eyes are always closed. Everything is happening at the same time. I decided it would be best to ask Bob to stop digging with me. He was more of a nuisance than an assistant. He doesn't know how to use a pick, he is not getting anywhere. All he does is hurt himself with it. I have lost my hope of finding the dead. The fourth pit is still empty. I go on digging so I can say that I dug right to the end. But I am sure the dead are not in the direction of the sunset. I ran into mud all of a sudden. I knew I would hit the sludge again if I continued. The sludge comes just after the mud. I preferred to stop before that. It is exactly like the second pit. The soil changes suddenly, and you run into mud. It must be because of the underground spring the father always used to talk about. There is a sort of vein of sludge running across the garden deep down, from east to west. All you have to do to find it is dig deep enough. The subsoil of the garden is made up of the ridge of rock in one direction and the vein of sludge in the other. There is no way I could have known. It is not a good kind of soil for the dead, even though it's lush and green on the surface. The dead are not in the rectory garden like I thought. I dug the pits, and they are all empty. I chose the wrong project. I don't know what to do anymore. The four walls of the church collapsed at the same time. It was to be expected, they have been crumbling for so long. All the stones that had fallen off finally took their toll on the parts that were still standing. The walls had not been solid for a long time. The father never maintained his church. He didn't open his eyes to see what was happening when what was left of the church collapsed. There is nothing but a pile of stones where it used to stand. It is a big pile, but you can see that it was not a church like the father used to say in order to make an impression. It was only a little chapel. Maybe that's why there are no dead there. The dead are next to churches like in the valley below, not next to chapels. I straightened up the pile of stones. It is almost in the center of the four pits.

The father never opens his eyes anymore. He lives in darkness. I can't feel his pulse. He must be in a coma. When I put the mirror in front of his mouth, it fogs up. That proves the father is in a coma. It must be what they call a deep coma. The father can't stay in his wheelchair anymore. I put him back in his bed. Now that I am done digging the pits, he can stay in bed. That's where he is most comfortable. He doesn't react. He is not suffering. He was suffering before, when I was looking for the dead and he was hoping I would find them. I never leave the father anymore. I have nothing more to do in the garden. Bob is never here. He must not want to be the father's assistant. Maybe he should have been a customs officer. He hasn't had an attack since he has been living in Forever Valley. He is right to say he can live with his lesion. Maybe he was cut out to live on the border in a customs office. The only thing that interests him in Forever Valley is the mountains overlooking the hamlet, and the path that leads to the pass and the border. He is not cut out for living in the rectory. The proof is that he is never here.

§11
This is the fifth Saturday, and yet it is a day like any other. There is no more dancehall. I have no more pits to dig. Bob asked me to come with him. He is going up to the

pass for the first time. He says he is feeling well, the air in the mountains of Forever Valley is good for his heart. He

says you must be able to see all of Forever Valley from the pass. The border is there too. Bob is curious to see what the border looks like at the top of the pass. I told Bob I didn't want to go up to the pass. The path is too steep and it is too high. In any case, I can't leave the father, who is still in a deep coma. Bob left by himself. He told me he would be back before evening. He has not forgotten that today is Saturday. He seems happy. He looks well.

I watched over the father all morning. The father is motionless in his bed. At noon, I put the mirror in front of his mouth, like every day at noon since he went into the coma. I had a shock. But I should have expected it. There was no trace of fog on the mirror. The father is dead. He died of total paralysis. He died little by little without my noticing, while I was looking for the dead in the pits. I have always lived with the father. It never occurred to me that he might die one day. Even when he was completely paralyzed, I still didn't think he could die. He is dead now that there is no more fog on the mirror. And Bob isn't even here. The father is nothing to Bob. I have no right to be angry with him for not being here. The rectory doesn't really mean anything to Bob, all that matters is the pass. I prepared the father's body. The wheelchair will not be of any use now. It was a bad wheelchair. It will not even be worth selling at auction. It's like the harmonium no one wanted. I am going to bury the father in the first pit, the one on the north side, the first one I dug. The father was full of hope back then, he thought I was going to find the dead in no time. He was so excited he almost thought he was the one digging. He criticized me for not knowing how to dig. The first pit was his favorite. It's a good thing there is rock at the bottom of the pit. It will be a very solid grave.

I put the father in the wheelchair one last time. I pushed the wheelchair out to the garden, as I have done so often. This time, the father is dead. I wanted to wheel him around the garden one last time. We made a few circles around the garden, very gently, so he would not be jolted. I hesitated for a long time before I stopped in front of the first pit. It's hard for me to bury the father where I dug. And yet I have to do it. Finally I laid the father at the bottom of the pit, right on the rock. And then I went and got my shovel. And I filled in the pit. It was a great deal of work filling it in. It took all my strength. It is harder to fill in a pit than to dig one. It took me hours to fill in the pit, it was so deep. It was the father's idea to dig it so deep. I would never have run into the rock otherwise. The father had his reasons. Now that the pit is filled in, it is no longer a pit. It's a grave. I surrounded it with stones from the church so it would be even more of a grave. I don't know how to write. Otherwise I would have written the father's name on the biggest stone, which I put just at the end so it would be like a gravestone. I regret not knowing how to write. Because of me, the father won't have his name on his grave. I stayed beside the grave for a long time, waiting for Bob to come back. He will hardly notice that the father is dead. All he will see is that there are only three pits in the garden.

I went to meet Bob. I put on my organdy dress with flounces and my patent leather high heels, since it's Saturday night. I don't have any mourning clothes. Bob will be happy to see that I did not forget to dress before coming to meet him. It is Saturday night, after all, even if the father is dead and there is no more dancehall. I put on my second dress, because I got the first one dirty sleeping by the edge of the third pit with Bob last Saturday. Massi was right to say you should always have a spare dress. I couldn't go on sitting alone by the father's grave and waiting for Bob. I hardly recognize the rectory. Without the father, I don't know what the rectory is. It looks onto the garden where the father is buried, and it used to look onto the church. I thought Bob must not be far away. But I did not meet him like I hoped. He must have lingered at the pass instead of coming back down before the end of the afternoon like he had promised me. And yet Bob keeps his word. Then I was afraid. I thought of his lesion. Bob never talked about it anymore because he had not felt ill since he had been living in Forever Valley. But his lesion is still there. The path that goes up to the pass is steep. Bob might have begun to feel faint. Even the dancehall was enough to make him feel faint. With this sun, if he began to feel faint, that would be a real problem.

I used to say I would never climb such a steep path. I am not wearing the right shoes. But I climbed it anyway to look for Bob. It's covered with gravel that shifts under your feet. I twisted my ankles in my patent leather high heels. They were made for the dance floor, not for the path that leads to the pass. Bob must have had a hard time climbing. It is not the kind of path you should climb if you have a heart lesion. I didn't see Bob on the path. I thought again that he must be feeling faint, otherwise I would have met him. I climbed faster than I have ever climbed, although I have never been to the pass in my life. All that digging has made me tougher. All the same, it took me about an hour to get to the pass. The sun was just setting. Bob wasn't lying. All of a sudden, I saw Forever Valley. That showed I was getting near the pass. I will never forget the sight of Forever Valley from the pass at sunset. It was all pink, in a kind of fog. I could not enjoy the sight for long. Right away I saw Bob stretched out on the ground unconscious. I was right to be afraid as I climbed the path. The climb was too steep for him, especially at the end. He could not have predicted that it would become so steep at the end. Pushing himself so hard to get to the top made him feel faint. With the sun beating down, he lost consciousness. He must have sunstroke. I did everything I could to bring him around. I gave him heart massage. I gave him mouth-to-mouth resuscitation. But I didn't get anywhere. And

yet I could feel his heart beating, that was a good sign. The father always told me I had no talent for massages.

It was not easy to come back down the path with Bob. I had a hard time supporting him. I almost had to carry him. Bob doesn't weigh much, but he is still too heavy for me. I fell several times on the path, and Bob fell with me. We rolled downhill, with me clinging to Bob. I don't know how far he might have rolled if I had let go of him. The slope is steep. An unconscious body can pick up speed. There is nothing to hold you back on the slope. One of my shoes fell off. It rolled away, I couldn't catch it. I had to take off the other shoe. I came down barefoot. Bob and I are both covered with bruises from having rolled down the path from the pass. My organdy dress is all torn. It is no longer wearable. I don't know how I managed to get to the rectory. It was almost dark. Towards the end, I was dragging Bob. I couldn't support him anymore, so I dragged him. He has little wounds all over his body. I was right never to want to climb the path. I never even saw the border at the top of the pass. Maybe Bob saw it, and I just couldn't recognize it. Bob is used to borders, I am not. Why did he want to climb up to the pass? He has already seen the border in the valley below, it's the same one that runs through the pass. When we got to the rectory, I laid Bob on the bed. He was still unconscious. I washed him

carefully. I disinfected all his wounds. They are not deep wounds. They will heal quickly. It didn't even occur to me to wash myself, or to disinfect myself where I was bleeding.
I kept my organdy dress on, even though it was all torn. I only have one shoe left. I will never to go the dancehall again. Even in the dancehall, it always took Bob a long time to come around. We are not in the dancehall now.

All of a sudden I noticed that Bob was very white. I took his pulse, and didn't feel anything. His heart wasn't beating anymore. Bob had heart failure. Maybe it happened on the way down from the pass, with all the times we fell. That might have caused a congestion. His heart was still beating when we were at the pass, because I felt his pulse. And now his heart has stopped beating. Bob said he could live with his lesion. He was wrong. It was fatal. The proof is that he is dead. He should have gone to live far from the border. In Forever Valley the border is too close and the path that leads to the pass is too steep. It attracted Bob. He died because of it. I had hoped he would get used to the rectory. The father was used to it, and so was I. Bob is the only person I have ever known who didn't come from Forever Valley. I never really knew officers Fred and Ted. And now Bob is dead. I did not want him to die. I would have liked for him to live in the rectory with me.

I carried Bob out to the third pit. I did it almost automatically. I dragged him more than I carried him. What does it matter now that he is dead? This is the pit we slept by on Bob's first night at the rectory. That was just last Saturday. This is the only pit that looks towards the pass. That is the one Bob would have chosen. I did exactly like I did with the father. I put Bob right on the rock. It's the same rock as in the father's grave. This time I did it at night, instead of in full sunlight. There is a full moon, and stars, like the other night when Bob and I slept by the edge of the pit. I spent the night burying Bob, filling in the pit with dirt. I picked up the dirt in my hands. I never want to use the shovel again. When the pit was filled in, I didn't surround it with stones like the father's grave. I don't want Bob's grave to look like the father's, even if they are symmetrical, one to the north and the other to the south. Soon there will be no way to distinguish between Bob's grave and the garden. The grass will cover it over. The father's grave will always have the stones from the church to mark its edges. That is how I wanted it to be.

I will never be able to forget this fifth Saturday. The rectory garden is no longer a garden, it is a cemetery. As day broke, I thought of the bad luck that had come my way because I wanted to look for the dead. The dead are there in the rectory garden now, at the bottom of the first and third pits. I thought again about what Massi had said about the dead. Maybe she was right to say that you should never look for them. I stayed by Bob's grave for a long time. I cried for the first time. From Bob's grave, I can

see the father's. I see it clearly because of the stones sur-
rounding it. There was no way I could have known I was
digging graves when I was digging the pits. I thought the
dead were already there. I will never dig another pit.

I could not stand to see the two empty pits full of mud and
sludge and attracting insects. So I filled them in with the
stones from the church. The stones from the church are
the best thing for filling in empty pits. The pile of stones
was much smaller once I had finished filling in the two
pits. You would never guess there used to be a church in
the rectory garden. The pile of stones is too small to make
a church, even the very smallest church. When I was finished filling in the two empty pits, I slept like a log.

§12

I went to see Massi in the rest home to tell her about the
father's death, and Bob's as well. I don't feel at home anymore in the empty rectory. I don't feel at home anywhere
in Forever Valley now, without the father or Massi. I
spend my days by Bob's grave. That cannot continue.
Massi was right. The rest home is a beautiful building,
even bigger than the dancehall. Massi is having a hard
time becoming acclimated to the valley below. She is having respiratory problems. It must be because of the change
in altitude. She said nothing when I told her the father
and Bob were buried in the rectory garden. She doesn't
want to talk about it. She wanted to show me her bun-

galow. It was built quickly. She was not lying when she said it would almost build itself. It is a tiny bungalow with only one floor, for just one person. It's varnished inside and out. It seems tiny compared to the dancehall. Massi told me it was all she could afford. It's the smallest model of bungalow there is. She showed me around. It has all the modern conveniences. It is all electric. I don't see the point of that, since there is no electricity in the valley below and the generator from the dancehall is beyond repair. Massi said the valley below will have electricity soon. She does not seem to miss the dancehall. The girls from the dairy come to see her at the home. Massi thinks they are not the same anymore. There is a new dancehall in the valley below where the herdsmen go on Saturday nights. The girls from the dairy were not hired there, their time is past. It is just like I thought, the closing of the dancehall was a very bad thing for them. Massi has forgotten about the head customs officer. She has forgotten about all the customs officers. She wants to forget about Forever Valley. She took me to the cemetery to see the mayor's grave, which she has had redone. His tomb is almost as big as the bungalow. It's like a mausoleum. Now I understand why Massi only had enough money to build the smallest model of bungalow. She spent almost all she had for a new tomb for the mayor of Forever Valley. It is the most beautiful one in the cemetery. You can see it from far away. The mayor's name and the name Forever Valley are written on the stone in big letters. Massi read them to me several times. She showed me the place where her name will go. She will be buried with her husband, the mayor of Forever Valley. She is thinking ahead. It soothes her to know she has a place reserved for her next to the mayor in such a beautiful tomb. I offered to help her move into her bungalow. She told me she would rather wait a while longer. She is very happy in her room in the home because of the panoramic view. It's a big room with a bathroom, like my room in the dancehall. Massi appreciates the comfort of the home. From her room she can see everything that happens in the valley below. She lives on the second floor of the home. There is a lot of activity in the valley below. The herds are healthy again. The girls from the dairy are much too busy to think about the dancehall. They are going to get old quickly.

I went back to see Massi every day. I cannot stay by myself in the rectory any longer. I get terrified like the father used to when he dreamt about the dead. And yet I am not dreaming about the dead. In the garden, the grass and the plants are growing back over the graves and the pits. It is a cemetery, but soon people will think it's only a garden. I don't like the rectory garden anymore. Forever Valley is nothing but a cemetery now. Massi told me about the project of the mayor of the valley below. He wanted to do something to make up for the closing of the customs office. He doesn't want the valley to be cut off from everything. He had the idea of building a dam to make electricity. He brought in a team of specialists. He compared the various plans. And then he chose the one best suited to the valley below. They will build a dam just at the edge of Forever Valley. The whole hamlet will be submerged, right up to the foot of the mountains. The water will come from Forever Valley's underground lake. It is not a spring like the father used to think, it's a big lake. Once they tap it, it will provide water for the reservoir. Massi approves of the mayor's project. The valley below will finally be able to modernize. Massi will be reimbursed for her dancehall. That way she will have some savings again. She will not be left with nothing. That comforts her. She told me I couldn't live at the rectory anymore. I will not be reimbursed like Massi. The rectory doesn't belong to me. Massi said it was the best thing for me to be leaving Forever Valley now that everything is empty. I don't know if I could have gone on living there. I cannot bear the sight of the graves in the garden.

Massi took care of me. She wanted me to live in her bungalow. In the end she prefers the home, because it's bigger and she is on the second floor. There is no view from the bungalow. Massi says the bungalow is just right for me. I feel lost in the valley below. Massi's bungalow is the only place I can live. Massi told me I would have to start working again to make a living. I was afraid she would tell me about the new dancehall where the herdsmen go on Saturday night. I don't want to work in a dancehall anymore.

Massi had an idea, but it was not the dancehall. It wasn't the dairy either. Massi knows I would never be able to bear that. She knows I can't read and that I have no ambition. She wants to teach me to sew. She has gone back to spending her afternoons the way she used to. She sews dresses for the girls of the valley below. She has established a new clientele. The girls from the dairy never get dressed up anymore now that they have stopped going to the dancehall. The girls from the valley below come to the home for fittings. Massi's room has become a little workshop. Massi has changed designs. She doesn't make straight slit sateen dresses anymore, because they are not the right style for the girls of the valley. She uses designs that suit them. She doesn't make organdy dresses anymore because they are out of fashion, and the girls of the valley below want to be dressed fashionably. Massi does good work. She never lacks orders. She could give up sewing and live on her savings after they reimburse her for the dancehall. But she wants to keep up some kind of activity. She needs a helper. That's why she is teaching me to sew. I am her apprentice. I do the preliminary work and the finishing touches. Massi never thinks about her own appearance now that she is making dresses for the girls of the valley below. She wants me to dress just like them, because she says I am also from the valley below now that I have left Forever Valley. Massi's new dresses don't suit me. They are not my style. They are not like the organdy dresses with flounces. But Massi decided for me. I wouldn't know how to make a dress with flounces all by myself. I am only an apprentice. It is hard to learn how to sew, almost as hard as learning to read. But I make every effort to learn. I have to make a living, and I have to pay Massi rent for the bungalow. The father didn't leave me anything. He lived on his savings. That was what he raised me on, and he used them all up. I don't have the necessary abilities for sewing. I try to do what Massi shows me. I have no initiative. Massi is not demanding. She just needs a helper. Massi's big reward, and the proof that her reputation in the valley below was established, was when the mayor's wife came to buy a dress from her. Massi showed her her most beautiful dresses. Now she also makes dresses for the mayor's daughters. Massi invents her most beautiful designs for them. She never talks to me about Forever Valley. I never talk to her about it either.

The dam was officially opened. It supplies electricity to all of the valley below. Massi bought herself an electric sewing machine with the money she was reimbursed. The dam is a victory for the mayor. The dairy has modernized, it runs on electricity. That makes things easier for the girls from the dairy. They built a paved road instead of the gravel road that went up from the valley below to Forever Valley. There is a big sign just at the entrance to the road. It says in big letters: FOREVER VALLEY DAM. Dam is the second word I have learned to read, after dancing. I don't sew for Massi on Sundays, it's my day off. I put on my organdy dress, the one I got dirty sleeping by the edge of the pit with Bob. The other one was so torn up I had to throw it away. When I washed my dress, all the sizing that was left in it washed out. The flounces aren't crisp at all now. Too bad if it's not a fashionable dress anymore. I put on flat shoes. They are more comfortable for climbing up to the dam, even if they don't really go with my organdy dress. I don't know how I felt when I saw that the hamlet was no longer there. I saw an expanse of water where it used to be. They say it is very deep. I threw in the patent leather high-heeled shoe left over from the dancehall. I can't do anything with one shoe. It sank right away. It must be deep. The water has a dark color because of the mountains reflected in it. Everything gets mixed up inside my head when I look at the water in the reservoir and tell myself that down on the bottom there is the hamlet, there is the garden which is a cemetery, there is the father's grave and Bob's grave. Bob was not from the hamlet. But he didn't know where to go. He said yes right away when I asked him to come and live at the rectory, as if that was what he wanted. I spend hours looking at the water. No matter how much I look, I can never see the bottom. All I see is the mountains reflected in the water, and the path leading up to the pass. Forever Valley is completely submerged now. To think that there used to be nothing but rock at Forever Valley, except for the rectory garden, and now there is nothing but water.

I am not sixteen anymore. But I am still not developed. Massi says it is too late now, I never will be developed. She can't understand why, since my anatomy is normal. I can't get used to the valley below. All the appliances in the bungalow are working since there is electricity now. I don't use them much. This is Massi's bungalow. I am only a tenant. I earn my living by sewing. I live apart from the valley below. Massi doesn't seem to realize that I don't like sewing, and I don't like the bungalow either. Everything smells like the dairy. Even though the dairy is all electric, it is still same smell. Massi's respiratory problems have disappeared. She is perfectly acclimated to the new altitude. The doctor at the home found I was anemic. He gave me some tonic. But I can't tolerate tonic anymore. Bob had a lesion. I can get along with anemia. I never go with Massi to the cemetery of the valley below. I don't like the dead, or the graves. I don't like the valley below either, or the Forever Valley dam with the mountains reflected in the water and the pass that you see just at the bottom, where the former hamlet of Forever Valley is hidden.

Interview

Q: You have written that the complexity of your writing plays itself out 'in some area other than what is known in the French literary tradition as style.' And yet there is in all your writing a very distinctive style (or perhaps a language, a tone – a manner of expression, at any rate), an almost monumental style, and one which signifies something, like any style. To what extent does your manner of writing seem necessary to you? In other words, would it be possible to tell the stories you tell in some way other than you do?

A: No, I'm sure that it would be impossible to tell the stories I tell in some other way. It is after all the writing (what you call the style) that contains the fiction, it is the writing that creates meaning. When I am not engaged in the process of writing, I know nothing of the story I am going to write, and when I have begun to write, I know nothing of what will follow. Often, the story to be told lies hidden in names (titles, place names, names of characters). The style contains everything, in a way. It becomes a style when it succeeds in capturing imagination and reality, when it has found the necessary tone to make of them a living story incarnated in language.

What I meant in the text you mention is that my style is in a state of rupture, of radical otherness, in relation to what French literature calls style, according to the grand tradition, of which the *Nouvelle Revue Française* is the guardian. But isn't any style, when it carries a world inside itself, in a state of rupture or scandalous otherness in relation to what tradition calls style?

Q: Despite the almost total absence of description in your books, I can see places and objects very clearly as I read: the snow-covered swamp in *Hôtel Splendid,* the pits in the rectory garden in *Forever Valley,* the square surrounded by pink buildings in *Rose Mellie Rose.* I wonder if there might be painters who have particularly influenced your visual imagination? Or filmmakers?

A: You raise a very important issue. The style that I have just referred to might have that very power, a poetic power to make visible that which has been neither described nor expressed by metaphor, but rather only evoked. As if the language that I had to invent carried inside it, within its structure, this hallucinatory power of sight. The reader creates the film of the story as he or she reads, a private cinema. This requires a release of the imagination if the book is not to remain forever closed to the reader. It is probably no coincidence that – starting with *Rose Mellie Rose* – photographs, and later on movies, are a part of the story, create a story within the story.

I could not say that certain painters or filmmakers have influenced my visual imagination, which comes from poetry. What my writing tries to do is to appropriate the power of the photographic image and especially the cinematic image. This allows the writing to capture the real, to make it visible. But the fact that the image is born of the power of language alone means that it is not only an image, but also a thought that creates meaning.

I would like that to be my revenge as a writer, at a time when we are entering into a culture of the all-powerful image, which threatens to kill literature: to invent a language that would be capable, by liberating the vital forces of imagination and thought, of resisting the images – seductive, manipulative, stultifying, and alienating – that invade us from all sides.

Q: Your books are, very clearly, written in the feminine mode: narrated by women, they privilege links (of friendship, of family) between women. To what extent are these feminist texts? Where do you situate yourself in relation to feminism?

A: It's true that in the triptych (but not in the three books – poetry, stories, theater – that preceded it), it is a woman who narrates the story of which she is at the same time the heroine. As if the novel could only have begun for me through these female voices, coming from some hidden depth, like the isolated sites in which the narrators live, and like the stories they tell.

Written in 1985–86, the triptych comes after the great period of feminist struggle and the writings that illustrated it. I think the triptych could only have been written afterwards, as a way of transforming all that history into fiction, becoming its legend. In the triptych, it is the women who fight, who seek, who create. The men are either decrepit and suicidal (Bob, Yem) or completely assimilated into their social function (the railway workers, the herdsmen and the customs officers, the secondhand man of Oât). The triptych tells of a violent cultural crisis between men and women, at a time when women, through their emancipation, were forging a history. In the books that follow the triptych, the relations between men and women evolve, so that a new history can be written. My relationship to feminism? I work as a woman, for men and for women, in order to write a new history through a farewell to the old.

Q: The swamp and the lavatories in *Hôtel Splendid,* the dam in *Forever Valley,* the lagoon, the ocean, the falls in *Rose Mellie Rose:* water is a theme that constantly returns in the triptych (and in your other texts), and generally in a rather ambiguous manner: for instance, the water of the Hôtel Splendid is at the same time beneficial for the stomach and damaging to the skin. What does water represent in your writings?

A: Yes, water – almost completely absent from my first three books – becomes very present in the settings of the triptych. In *Hôtel Splendid* it is an omnipresent and all-powerful force: the devouring swamp, which carries violence and death. And the lavatories you mention never stop becoming blocked, making the hotel uninhabitable until the narrator, who has spent her life unblocking them, decides to give up on them and go back to the bucket, which she empties into the swamp as a sort of placatory offering. Only at the end does the frost put a stop to the murderous power of the swamp, through a sort of immobilization of time. Where modern knowledge and technology (by way of the railroad company) fail to tame the swamp, the narrator, with a very different sort of knowledge and technology, succeeds – but at the price of an almost Christ-like sacrifice of her life to her hotel.

In contrast, the setting of *Forever Valley* is rocky and sterile, except for the hidden spring that lies, according to the father, under the rectory garden. In this death-haunted place, the narrator looks not for the spring but for the dead, and what she finds as she digs is a vein of sludge. By building the dam, the valley below succeeds in tapping the spring and the underground lake that feeds it, in order to provide water for the reservoir that drowns Forever Valley. Modern knowledge and technology succeed this time, but only by putting the site of Forever Valley to death. A violent contradiction appears within the forces of civilization: the origin of a new conflict, of which water is, in a way, the metaphor (political conflict having its roots in primitive and symbolic conflicts).

Only in *Rose Mellie Rose* does water appear in several forms. The swamp reappears, calmer now, in the form of the lagoon of Oât, a stagnant and dying water, like the neighborhood that borders it. For the first time, there is also a living water, the falls of the Hermitage, where Mellie played as a little girl and where she finally returns to give birth to Rose. The sea appears for the first time as well, and it will continue to reappear from book to book after *Rose Mellie Rose.* The place of poetic and mythic quests, the sea is also a radical appeal to desire. With the sea returns the temptation evoked by Rimbaud, in the form of the *Queen of the Fairies* and the channel in which she becomes lost. After the triptych it will be necessary to cast off this temptation. In *Silsie,* which can be read as an epilogue to the triptych, the channel is replaced by the center of the ocean, toward which the lifeboat moves. A myth of death gives way to a myth of rebirth. After *Silsie,* the ocean remains as a necessary and vital boundary, a transcendent appeal to a poetic and mythic quest, a quest that one must resist undertaking in order to imbue it with a symbolic existence. Unlike the swamp of the first novel, an archaic and barbarous divinity, the ocean is a blessed divinity, provided that one is able to keep one's distance from it and resist its deadly fusional appeal. In *Rose Mellie Rose,* the sea is also the place of a vital departure (the boat that links Oât with the continent), by which one leaves a doomed place.

Q: There is another theme that recurs very frequently: that of the double. Of all your books, *Doublures* is probably the most marked by this phenomenon, but it plays a role in the triptych as well. In *Hôtel Splendid,* Ada and Adel resemble each other, and in her last words Adel calls the narrator Ada. In *Rose Mellie Rose* there are several Roses and many Mellies, as well as many references to translations, mirrors, photos, paintings, all sorts of things that double or represent something else. For Freud, the double is linked to the *Unheimliche,* the Uncanny; is that the role that it plays in your books, or does it have a completely different meaning for you?

A: All these doubles you mention – the whole question of the double is very important in all my books, a question already clearly posed in the first three before the triptych. In *Le Mort & Cie,* when there is doubling (the dwarf and the smallest dwarf), there is also an attempt at using the double not in a twin relationship or in a play of mirrors, but rather in a political or metaphysical dialectic of difference: the master and the king, God and the dead man. In confronting these situations, the characters (the dwarf, the smallest dwarf, the jester) become able to play, to become autonomous, to move. Immediately after *Le Mort & Cie, Doublures* depicts a hellish doubling and failed attempts to escape it. Although sexual difference appears for the first time here, through the alternating play of names and stories (Lia, Lii, Gem, Gim, Sil, Sim, Gal, Gil, Lam, Lim, Nel, Nil), each sex remains distinct from the other, closed inside its own story of doubling, a story that returns with the murderous family of *Tir et Lir,* locked inside a monstrous and deadly twinning.

The triptych poses the same question again, and for the first time the answer is linked with creation: a movement from the Hôtel Splendid to the Splendid, from Forever Valley to the valley below, from the old Rose to the new-born Rose, a movement that introduces an idea of meta-morphosis, of departure, of a transmission of difference. That is what is at stake in the triptych. The mirroring that you mention represents confusion, loss, and death. The narrators, through the power of their 'I,' of their radically singular voice, fight against the proliferation of the dou-ble; they try to find a name, an identity, by creating a work of their own. To the mirrors and the faded portraits in the old houses of Oât, Mellie opposes her Polaroid that pho-tographs the people around her in all their otherness, which she symbolizes with the legends she writes on the backs of the photos. Thus it is a question of using the work of writing to introduce the other into the double, which is at the same time sexual, symbolic, political, and meta-physical, to escape from the repetitive circle of the double and its infinite variations, to enter into history and to create history.

While the double is, as you say, the Uncanny that Freud talks about, in my writing I start from that strangeness in order to leave it and to enter into another one, that of otherness from the world and from the other. The double leads back only to itself, infinitely, until death. Leaving behind the double means trying to leave behind – after having told its story – the psychosis of which the literature of modernity was, with Beckett, to die.

Q: Reading the triptych, one sometimes catches a glimpse of something like a rigorous structure; the rhythm of *Forever Valley*, for example, is punctuated by the cycle of Saturdays, Massi's visits, and the immutable order in which the narrator receives the customs officers. What role does structure play in the creation of your books?

A: What you call structure or composition is indeed a determining factor. Each book adheres to a rigorous structure, at the same time mathematical, architectural, and musical, which transforms itself from book to book: the elements multiply, the combinatorial system grows richer, space and thus mobility become more important, the story grows more complex. This structure is part of the language that I invented for myself in order to write, a language built from a lexical and syntactic emptiness that I had to impose on language. Maybe this very idea of structure takes the place of that lost rhetoric, becoming a means of generating another language, and thus another history.

Q: In discussing your books with you, I was struck by the frequency with which you laugh as you talk about them. What importance do you ascribe to humor in your writing?

A: A great importance, as in life. There is a kind of humor specific to each book (dark in *Hôtel Splendid*, lighter in *Rose Mellie Rose*). Humor is play, freedom, insolence, and intelligence, against the crushing weight of evil,

pain, and stupidity. It allows liberation from the mortal danger of identification. It is a refusal of pomp, of great
sentiments, of great ideas. But to humor I add poetry, which is love, dreams, and songs.

Q: Do your books express a philosophy? A way of seeing? Some critics have seen in your books a sort of allegory; do you agree?

A: A philosophy? It can only be contained within my books, seeking itself from book to book. But there are values, those of the ethic that my writing defends: the need for thought, the passionate desire for a profound emancipation of mankind, a love of life born of the torments of neurosis and pain, a revolt against and a resistance to the forces of death that ravage the world, a fight for the progress of civilization and the invention of a new History, the preservation of transcendence through the force of poetry, after coming to terms with the death of God and thus of all Utopias.

An allegory? Isn't all literature a fable, of life and the world?

Q: What is the role of autobiography in your books?

A: It is part of the raw material from which I create my work, without which it could never be built; but my work metamorphoses it, surpasses it, makes of it another story which is no longer only my own story. The story of the work doubles my autobiography in order to transcend it.

Q: Why do you write?

A: Perhaps I could first say why, at the age of about thirty, after my father's death, when I had no vocation to be a writer, I began to write: because in order to try to reinvent myself (out of the need to say my goodbyes to my own history and to that of my generation, born after the war), I could find no other way out than to forge a language and a history with my words. It was a vital necessity, stronger than I was.

Next, after the triptych, once the work had begun to take shape, to be recognized and socialized, my identity as a writer ripened little by little. In order to rebuild my life, I had to pursue the work which had begun to ground me and which was giving me a new social identity, that of a writer. By rebuilding my life, I continue my work. Literature is also my way of resisting everything that revolts me in my society and in the world, of defending the values I live for. More consciously than at the beginning (when the project was above all one of 'saving myself'), I see literature as an act with a political dimension.

Translated by Jordan Stump

In the European Women Writers Series

The Delta Function
By Rosa Montero
Translated by Kari A. Easton
and Yolanda Molina Gavilan

Music from a Blue Well
By Torborg Nedreaas
Translated by Bibbi Lee

Nothing Grows by Moonlight
By Torborg Nedreaas
Translated by Bibbi Lee

Forever Valley
By Marie Redonnet
Translated by Jordan Stump

Hôtel Splendid
By Marie Redonnet
Translated by Jordan Stump

Rose Mellie Rose
By Marie Redonnet
Translated by Jordan Stump

Why Is There Salt in the Sea?
By Brigitte Schwaiger
Translated by Sieglinde Lug

The Same Sea As Every Summer
By Esther Tusquets
Translated by Margaret
E. W. Jones